LONE TREE

WISDOM - HUMOR - THE GREAT DEPRESSION

LONE TREE

WISDOM - HUMOR - THE GREAT DEPRESSION

Robert W. Lamb

RWL BOOKS
Puerto Vallarta, Jalisco

Granddad used to say, "Everybody who wants to be in Lone Tree is already here, and nobody passing through ever changes their mind."

8

ACKNOWLEDGEMENTS

My wife, Carolyn: *Your loving encouragement was essential for me during the process of writing this book.*

My daughter Kim: *This book never would have existed had not you convinced me that a story teller could also be a writer.*

My stepdaughter, Suzanne: *Your critical eye and attention to detail in the final editing transformed a very rough draft into a manuscript.*

CONTENTS

A PLACE TO START

I was born on February 22, 1929 in a small house about a hundred yards in back of the Lone Tree Store. I was the oldest child, but not the firstborn.

My mother was eight months pregnant with her first child in the beginning of 1928 when she contracted a severe case of whooping cough. The constant coughing was an ordeal for her, but she was a young, healthy woman of twenty-two years, so she expected to tolerate the cough and give birth to her child on schedule, in approximately three weeks.

Dr. Thayer was not as optimistic. After giving my mother a variety of medicines including sassafras tea to help with the coughing, he asked her to send someone to the Lone Tree store to call him when she was ready to deliver. This unusual step was an indication of his concern, as a local midwife named Bessie Meyers was usually the only one to attend to births around Lone Tree.

On the day my older brother was born, my mother was so sick that she later recalled the pattern on the faded wallpaper seemed to be dancing. The baby was stillborn. He was wrapped in a blanket and buried behind the house. Only Granddad and my parents were present for the burial. There was no ceremony except for Mom's sobbing and Dad mumbling about having his first son torn from his life before he had a chance to live. There was no grave marker except a young oak tree a few feet away from the tiny mound of dirt. Before long, grass crept back over the fresh dirt of the grave. Only the oak tree was left as a reminder of a baby boy who paid the ultimate price for having been born into these harsh surroundings.

I was born almost exactly one year later, a healthy ten pounds and fourteen ounces. When he heard how much his new grandson weighed, Granddad said, "My God, Theoree, this kid was three months old when he was born! That don't happen much in these parts. Here when you plant somethin' you're lucky to get your seed back."

My three sisters were also born healthy. Elaine came two years later; Bonnie arrived four years after me; Janet was born two years after Bonnie.

Because I was born on February 22, Dr. Thayer wanted to name me George Washington Lamb, but Mom wouldn't hear of it. The name they gave me came from a fairly common source in Lone Tree: one grandfather was named Robert and the other, William, so the only decision was which name to place first.

Since Granddad McDonald, whose given name was Robert, lived closer than William Lamb, I was named Robert William, or as many called me, Bobby Bill. I was the only boy, which meant that all of the "men folks" chores would fall to my father and me. None of this would have happened without a double wedding that occurred years earlier.

A DOUBLE WEDDING

My mother, Theora, born in 1905, and her sister, Lora Mae, born a year earlier, were the only two children born to my grandparents, Robert and Myrtle McDonald. Both girls desperately wanted to continue their education, but their parents, especially Granddad were against it. "High school is a silly waste of time for girls. Them school people don't know anything that will help the girls to work hard and be good wives," Granddad would often say. I don't think Grandma agreed but she decided to let it pass rather than have a big argument with Granddad that she would lose.

Anyway, they were pretty girls with freckles and bright red hair. It would be no problem marrying them off.

My father, Alfred Ross Lamb, was the youngest and only boy in a family of five children. His mother died when he was eight-years-old, so the role of mother fell to his four older sisters: Icey, Jessie, Allie, and Annie.

Their parents, William and Marie Ellen, were born, grew up, and married in rural Eastern Kentucky. I only saw one photograph of my paternal grandparents, in which William was seated in a straight-backed chair and Marie Ellen stood beside him dressed in a long, black dress with a high neck and a bonnet, tied neatly under her chin. She was very thin, with dark hair, and deep-set, very sad eyes. Her maiden name was also Lamb. It was taken around 1900 in the yard of their small one story house, which had siding of unpainted boards and a shingle roof with several patches. The porch was barely large enough for the swing and the two homemade wooden chairs. The screen door was sagging too much to close completely so it remained too open to keep flies out but too closed to enter without a struggle.

William and Marie Ellen lived on a small farm where William worked with his father and four brothers in their logging business before moving to Champaign, Illinois. There my father and his four sisters were born. At the age of nineteen, Dad left William and Marie Ellen's farm and moved sixty miles away to a place called Lone Tree in southern rural Indiana. There, he planned to work during the wheat-harvesting season. When the harvest dwindled, he found part-time work on Granddad McDonald's farm, where he met my mother, Theora. He would never return to Illinois.

For two years, Ross and my future uncle, John Bays, toiled on the McDonald farm, then married the comely red-headed McDonald girls.

Their parents treated the sisters like twins, even holding Lora Mae back a grade so she could attend elementary school with Theora as a classmate. The wedding was to be no different. There was to be a double ceremony to wed Theora to Ross and Lora Mae to John. The wedding took place in Providence Baptist Church with the Reverend Charlie Welch presiding.

At last, they would be able to use the items they had stored so carefully in their hope chests since they were twelve and thirteen. The item each cherished the most was the multi-colored quilt that their grandmother, Millie Meese, had spent a year stitching with equal parts love and thread. They also had collected warm cotton sheets, wool blankets, nightgowns, and an assortment of pots and pans. Some were new, but most sported the patina of untold history.

Grandma Myrtle sewed each of the girls a simple white wedding dress with ruffles around the necks and hemlines. The ruffles would later be removed and the dresses worn for other less formal occasions such as church, fish fries, and ice cream socials. They didn't wear veils, but matching white hats, each pinned with a small nosegay of lilacs.

The attire of the two grooms was also nearly identical. They wore the only suits they owned. Both were brown and threadbare. Their wide ties were clipped onto the collars of their starched white shirts and their black shoes were newly polished.

Each had parted his hair in the middle and then made several unsuccessful attempts to control the unruly locks with generous applications of Brilliantine. Their rough, callused hands extended too far out of the sleeves of their shirts and seemed to twitch in the unfamiliar setting.

After all of the wedding participants gave their expected wooden performances, a wedding reception was held in Granddad and Grandma McDonald's back yard, where a picnic table groaned under the weight of numerous pies, cakes, and large glasses of homemade cider. Everyone wished the newlyweds long, happy lives. But most importantly, they wished them lots of babies.

That evening, after each couple had retired to their respective houses, they were accorded the customary honor of a "chivaree." This ritual involved standing outside the homes of the newlyweds and firing shotguns, yelling, and ringing cowbells. It usually took about an hour for the revelers to tire and lose interest in this noisy tradition. The wedding had no effect on the needs of the farm animals, so the next morning was business as usual. The couples had new titles, but their chores had not changed and would not change for decades. They would continue to act according to the unspoken custom in this farming community. They would work hard and have babies and grow old together.

LONE TREE

If I had not been born there, I, like most everyone else in the world, would never have heard of Lone Tree, Indiana. It did not qualify as a small town or even a village. It was just a crossing of two country roads marked by Saul Burchamp's store. There were no signs to tell you when you were entering or leaving Lone Tree. If you wanted to be there, you were and if you didn't, you weren't. This country community where I grew up during the grip of the Great Depression was not so much a community as a point in time and space where two dirt roads crossed before continuing on their separate ways.

The house in the grove of oak trees next to Saul's store where I spent the first five years of my life had about 600 square feet of floors of rough planks, flowered wallpaper, an upstairs and a downstairs. The two sources of heat, the fireplace and the kitchen stove, were both downstairs, and since my sisters and I slept in one of the two bedrooms upstairs, on cold winter mornings the routine was always the same: grab your clothes, race downstairs and dress in front of the fireplace. Mom would have already been in the kitchen for an hour to bring the banked fire to life so she could cook breakfast which often included eggs, fried squirrel, biscuits, or, if we were lucky, rabbit.

Everyone had their own version of how Lone Tree got its name; some old-timers credited an oak tree that grew directly in the path of the route chosen for the new gravel road in Smith Township. Nobody wanted to cut the tree down, so it became a local landmark as well as the inspiration for the community and everyone in it.

The larger of the two gravel roads running through Lone Tree was called "Lone Tree Road" and the other one was just the road that crossed it. Besides the tree, the only other landmark was Saul and Maggie Burchamp's store.

At first, it stocked only a few staples such as brown horehound candy; pork and beans; Cokes; and used comic books. As the years passed, they expanded and stocked some luxury items such as Spam and kidney beans.

Many local folks thought that Saul and Maggie were getting a little fancy when they installed a gas pump in front of the store. They fretted that Lone Tree was expanding too fast, running the danger of attracting foreigners from Indianapolis.

THE TREE

The arrangement with the tree in the middle of the road seemed to be fine with everybody except Granddad. For some reason he had a strong preference for driving around the tree on the left side. This didn't create a problem as long as he was alone on the road. This was usually the case in Lone Tree, but the specter of meeting another car on the left side of the tree while riding with Granddad in his 1935 yellow Packard worried me enough to ask him about it.

"It ain't a problem because everybody in these parts knows that I like the left side of the tree best," he said.

He must have been right, because he never had a wreck near the oak tree. The majority of his collisions occurred in the pastures where he would bump and rumble the car over rocks, shearing off bushes and shrubs as he drove out to get a closer look at a cow he was considering buying.

An afternoon of cow shopping frequently left the fenders on his Packard badly battered and hanging loose. Every two months, or so, Granddad had to make a trip to Linton, six miles away, to get his fenders reattached. The blame for the condition of his car, however, was always assigned to the rocks and bushes.

GRANDDAD:
A LONE TREE LEGEND

Granddad was a big man, standing six feet, one inch tall and weighing 230 pounds. He was quiet but he projected a presence that few could ignore. He had a kind face and a fringe of dark hair that surrounded a shiny pate, which he protected from the sun with a soft-brimmed brown hat.

Granddad came to Lone Tree as a young man with few assets beyond energy and ambition. His pay for his first job digging a well for a local farmer was a skinny calf. By the time he finished this lengthy task, the calf had doubled its weight while enjoying the farmer's lush pasture. He traded the fat calf for two skinny ones, thus discovering that selling things for more than you paid for them was a distinct possibility as a livelihood.

This successful experience established a pattern that he would follow for the rest of his life. Granddad seemed to have that special talent it takes to get rich from dealing with his neighbors. He needed to take a big enough bite to make a profit, but not so much that he appeared greedy or dishonest. He was a master of maintaining this fine balance, becoming the wealthiest and the most influential man in the area. Even elected officials, such as the township trustee, never made any big changes without consulting Granddad.

Although he lived off his neighbors, he was always generous and kind. It was common for him to lend a milk cow to a family down on their luck, or a family with a small baby whose mother wasn't producing milk. He was gentle to a fault and had to be pushed to say anything bad about anyone, unless he was asked what he thought of Wilmer Blanton. Then he was unable to suppress his real feelings. After some stalling and kicking a rock around with the toe of his shoe he finally said, "Well, if you ordered a whole trainload of sons of bitches and the train pulled up and only Wilmer got off, you'd had got your money's worth."

Some of his beliefs were as intractable as the lone tree that stood in the center of the road. For example, his relatively fancy house on Lone Tree Road had a water pump and a sink, but no indoor bathroom. He didn't think it was decent to have a toilet inside the house. He thought this indoor toilet thing was just a passing fad that would quickly fade. Grandma finally convinced him to install an indoor toilet, but he only agreed to have one in the corner of the basement as far as possible from the main part of the house. It was a year before he developed any confidence that the contraption knew how to handle what he might put in it.

A FRIENDLY GAME
OF CHECKERS

Harley Clinger, a farmer from Dugger Township, had two Angus heifers for sale. Granddad liked the looks of the heifers but he wasn't too sure about Harley. He seemed to be a little too nervous and fidgety for a guy with such a big jolly body, but he had an honest face and his eyes weren't too shifty.

Granddad said, "A real smart feller once wrote that you can look into a person's eyes and see all the way to the soul, but I have found that a game of checkers is every bit as good when it comes to checking out the soul."

Granddad invited Harley to drop by the store after he finished his chores and they could talk about the heifers over a friendly game. Harley considered himself to be a pretty good player so he jumped at the chance to beat Bob McDonald at a game of checkers and sell him two heifers all at the same time. When Harley arrived, Granddad greeted him with a slight nod and pointed to the back where the checkerboard was set up on a nail keg between two wood chairs. Harley took a seat next to the red checkers and waited to begin his conquest. After a few minutes he began to show some signs of nervousness as Granddad continued to wander around the store while he cleaned the ashes from his pipe by knocking it against the side of the pot-bellied stove. Harley tried some small talk about the weather but got no response. When Granddad finally joined the game, Harley had beads of sweat on his forehead and his checker-moving finger was twitching. Granddad was already getting a little peek at Harley's soul.

After about fifteen minutes of trading black checkers for red ones, the game started to get more intense and four or five spectators gathered around to watch.

Granddad said, "Harley, do you feed them heifers any grain? They look purty skinny for this time of year." Without looking up from the checker board, Harley said, "They get a pile of soy bean every morning and the grass is real good in the south pasture."

Granddad said, "Well there must be some other reason why their eyes aren't shiny and their fur is dull."

At this point in the game Harley was sweating more and having trouble deciding on a good move, while Granddad didn't seem as concerned as he should have been. Just when things were looking pretty grim for Harley his luck changed for the better.

Granddad made a really dumb move: he let Harley have a double jump and go on to win the game. This was better than Harley had hoped for. His ego was soaring as he explained his brilliant strategy to the bystanders. In the midst of all the excitement Granddad said, "I'll give you seventy-five dollars for them two skinny heifers." Harley wanted at least a hundred dollars for them but at that moment he couldn't bear to break the spell of feeling like a winner, so he accepted the offer without hesitation.

The next day when I went with Granddad to collect the heifers, I asked him what went wrong in the checker game. His only response was a sly grin.

WHEN GRANDMA
WENT AWAY

I knew something was not right with Granddad as I watched through a frosty window while he got out of his car and walked towards the house. His pace was slow, his face was too serious, and his old brown hat was pulled all the way down to his ears. He was barely inside the door before he was telling Mom the reason for his early morning visit. "Your mom ain't at all well. I done called Doc Thayer and he is on his way out to the house, but I thought you ought to be there just in case he tells us something that we don't want to hear. As you know, your mom ain't one fer complainin', but she don't eat much and she's pale as a ghost."

Dad was left to milk the cows and feed the hogs, and in no time at all, Mom and I were in Granddad's yellow Packard on our way to his house. When we arrived, Doc Thayer was sitting in a chair beside Grandma, who was lying on her back with her eyes closed. When I went to the side of her bed she reached out to touch me, but never turned her head or opened her eyes. I thought she must be awfully sick because always before she would give me a nice long look and tell me how much I had grown and how big I was for a five-year-old. Mom had tears running down her cheeks as she put her hand on Grandma's forehead and just stared at her face for a long time.

Doc Thayer pointed to the living room and we went there so he could tell us about Grandma's sickness. After standing and looking at us for a long time, he removed his glasses and came over to stand in front of the sofa, where Mom and I were sitting on either side of Granddad. He said, "Things don't look too good for Myrtle. She is a fighter, but her heart doesn't sound strong enough to keep her going much longer. I can never be sure about these things, but I think it's time to tend to any unfinished business with her and let her start making her peace with the Lord a little ahead of time."

I never knew a room could be so quiet. Granddad put one hand on Mom's arm and cupped my chin with the other. No one moved for several minutes then Granddad turned to look at Mom then at me. He spoke finally. He said, "The people making up a family don't stay the same. Loved ones leave us before we are ready to turn them loose, and new ones arrive before we are ready for them. Over a long time we will have all new people, but we will still be the McDonald family. That's just how nature works. Myrtle is a wonderful mother and wife with a heart that is big enough to hold a lot of love, but not strong enough to keep her around much longer. When she passes on we will all hurt real bad for a long spell, but then we will heal and the family will go on like we always have."

The next time I saw Grandma her eyes were still closed but she had been moved from her bed into a shiny coffin in the living room.

FUNERALS:
A PRACTICAL APPROACH

Farmers deal with birth and death every day. There is always a cherished animal dying, so death, including that of people known and loved, was accepted as a natural event that was to be respected but not dwelled upon. The dearly departed took none of the problems on the farm with them, so concern was always focused on those left behind.

The coffin holding the deceased would rest on a piece of furniture that was of the appropriate height so the adults could check out the body, but children couldn't reach it. The dining room table was the typical choice for coffin placement, but Grandma's casket was placed on two sawhorses because the dining room table was needed for food.

The body was usually viewed for a day or two while the neighbors brought in lots of food to nourish the living members of the family. People viewing the body were always invited to eat during their visit, and I always wondered if some people didn't like the food better than the deceased. They were especially suspect if they visited more than once and arrived around mealtime.

Occasionally the family of departed one would use the Angel's Choice Mortuary in Linton. This arrangement allowed more room for the food at home and eliminated some of the freeloaders.

There was always concern focused on how natural the deceased appeared and if the clothes were really appropriate for the occasion. The midwife, Bessie Meyers, was the self-appointed critic of funerals. No one was certain about how well a funeral had gone until Bessie weighed in. Upon viewing my grandmother she remarked, "She looked purty natural, but that sure ain't her best dress. The blue one with the white collar would have looked a lot better. I guess they didn't want to bury her in her best shoes neither."

In spite of Bessie's fashion commentary, we all knew the unspoken rule about Lone Tree funeral wear: the departed loved one should be dressed in clothes nice enough to be remembered well, but not too nice to be given away forever.

The Lone Tree folks always liked to see a hint of a smile on the face of the departed. They felt that if you came into this world crying, you deserved to go out smiling.

THE SEARCH FOR THE GARDEN OF EDEN

The first time my family tried to leave Lone Tree was 1934. I was five-years-old, and the Great Depression had settled on the entire country. I was aware that our family didn't always have enough to eat, but I never considered us poor because we were just like everybody else in Lone Tree.

President Roosevelt helped people to survive by creating the *Public Works Act*, which put men to work repairing local roads. The men's wages were in the form of groceries delivered to their families every Saturday morning. One day of digging postholes on Granddad's farm would bring in another seventy-five cents in cash.

I guess we would have waited out the years of the Depression on our farm in Lone Tree had Dad not read an article in the Sunday edition of the *Linton Lantern*. The article that would change our lives detailed a place in California called Bakersfield, where good wages were being paid for people to pick oranges.

For the next week, my parents spoke of nothing but Bakersfield. Dad was certain our lives would be better there, but Mom dreaded the idea of leaving the only place she had ever known, especially because she was six months pregnant with my sister Janet.

She also had serious concerns about how a 1930 Model A Ford could hold a family with three children five and under, eighteen-year-old cousin Lester, and all of our belongings.

Dad's argument for leaving Lone Tree ultimately triumphed over Mom's desire to remain in familiar surroundings. Suddenly we were making plans to leave behind everything we had ever known for a chance at a better life in some faraway place that Dad had read about in a newspaper. Even at the age of five, I felt as if Mom was right.

Preparation for the trip took weeks. Horses, pigs and cows had to be sold and other items with which we could not bear to part were stored in Granddad's barn. I wouldn't miss the pigs very much, and I knew the cows would be happy with anybody who would feed them and relieve them of their heavy burden of milk every day.

I felt differently about my horse, Daisy. She had been my trusted friend all of my life. I told her how scared I was and her big brown eyes answered that she understood, but could not help.

I knew I couldn't take Daisy, but it was even sadder to learn that there would be no room in the car for most of our favorite things. After the agony of sorting eased somewhat, we were finally able to cram the remainder of our belongings into the trunk, with the exception of Cousin Lester's clothes, which were tied to the top of the trunk with a rope. Each of my sisters kept one rag doll and I was allowed to keep my toy car. My sisters cried each time they were told that something precious to them had to be left behind.

A week after we left Lone Tree, I got my first look at what would later be known as the Dust Bowl and the Okie migration. The newspaper article had failed to mention the terrible drought that had swept over the Southwest. Migrant workers from Oklahoma and other parts of the Midwest were streaming to California by the thousands, mattresses tied to the top of their sputtering, battered cars.

The parched land and abandoned farms showed no movement, except that from the warped doors being buffeted by the relentless wind. Sand had drifted against the withered buildings like brown snow.

Animal skeletons covered with nothing but weathered skins were strewn along the landscape, as if by some giant's hand. Eyes once bright and searching for green grass or water were now vacant, staring holes. I wondered what their last blurred image might have been. I thought this must be what Hell is like when nobody's home.

Driving through Devil's Canyon in Arizona was an unanticipated crisis for the entire family. No one was prepared for a ride on a narrow rocky road that hugged the side of the mountain. There was no guardrail between the road and a thousand-foot drop to the river.

Mom was sobbing and asking Dad how he could be so crazy as to bring the family to this God-forsaken place to die. My sister, Kibby, and I were spellbound, but Bonnie, as usual, retreated to the only place where she felt safe during tense times: the portable potty. With each day, the unity of the family seemed to erode as we found more reasons to question whether the Garden of Eden was actually located in Bakersfield.

The 'tourist cabins' where we spent nights were actually small wooden buildings with three or four cots and single light bulb dangling from the ceiling. One bathhouse served four or five cabins. The cost for lodging was fifty to seventy-five cents, depending on how close you were to the bathhouse and how many cots were in your cabin.

We finally arrived in Bakersfield about a week after leaving Lone Tree, having patched many inner tubes and having lost all of Cousin Lester's clothes. The reality of our situation began to dawn on us the very day we arrived. The Promised Land of sunshine and oranges was actually a labor camp crammed with desperate people living on hope and too few jobs picking fruit. There was at least one Okie for every unpicked orange.

Dad and Mom seemed to get a lot smarter almost overnight. We decided to drive back to Lone Tree while we still had enough money for the trip. Some of the new friends I had made envied our chance to return to a home, while others remained certain that prosperity was just beyond the next orange grove.

Dad and Mom still didn't see completely eye-to-eye on the decision to leave. Dad was certain things would improve, but Mom was determined to give birth to her baby in her own bed, assisted by the midwife, Bessie Meyers. Mom was sure that had Bessie been there for her first birth, I would have an older brother.

The trip home was comparatively uneventful save for the occasional flat tire and the tension between my parents. After we arrived home about a week later, we spent the first month back in Lone Tree living with Uncle Bob and Aunt Anna Waskom in Worthington while our furniture and belongings were retrieved and Mom and Dad found a house.

I was glad to be home. Most of all I was happy to be back with Daisy, but her big eyes told me that she knew the family that had returned was not the same one that had left.

PLOWING:
A TIME TO PLAN A LIFE

I was about seven when I had my first experience following a hand plow being pulled by two headstrong horses. I would tie the ends of the reins and loop them under my arms to free my hands to steer the horses. Sometimes the horses were too much for me and I'd fall and get dragged along behind the plow until the horses decided to stop on their own.

The field plowing probably had the most to do with the decision I had made early in life to someday leave Lone Tree, if only I could figure out how. I was reminded of that decision regularly, especially during two of the longest weeks of my thirteenth year.

It all began with Dad and Cousin Lester's decision to plant as much corn as Leonard Green did at his larger farm. Year after year, they coveted Leonard's huge corn harvest until they finally decided that there was no reason why they too could not become big-time operators.

They were well on their way with eighty acres of corn stalks standing about ten inches tall. All the green rows of corn needed were moisture and careful cultivation to produce a bumper crop in the fall. With the almanac predicting good rains, it all seemed possible. Plus, they had two tractors, each fitted with cultivator blades necessary to furrow down every row of corn, loosen the soil, and uproot any weeds. Lester's tractor had a bonus: a headlight in case of an emergency requiring us to work at night.

An emergency was on the way. The day before the gigantic task of cultivating was to begin, Lester fell off of a hay wagon, suffering a broken leg, Dad sprained his back taking Lester to Dr. Bork's office, and I was left, a thirteen-year-old, as the only able-bodied tractor driver.

Mom woke me every morning at six and fed me bacon and eggs, and I was on the tractor on my way to the cornfield by seven. I would spend the next several hours trying to keep the tractor between the rows of corn. Occasionally, in the early morning after a rain or heavy dew I would witness a scene that would occupy my mind for the remainder of the day.

As the sun would rise and the dew on the stalks of corn would glisten, the whole field of corn would come to life as if it had been rehearsed. I would be surrounded by popping sounds. It seemed that the little corn stalks were telling the world to wake up and look because they were doing something very special. I never told Dad about the popping corn because I knew he wouldn't believe such a tall story. The possibility of this experience made the morning trip to the cornfield less painful.

My mother would bring my lunch to the field where I would spend a half an hour under the shade of an oak tree eating sandwiches and talking to Mom.

With the hot sun and a belly full of lunch, it would take only about thirty minutes for my eyelids to become too heavy to bear. When I drove the tractor past the elm tree at the end of the field the lazy part of me said, "Stop and take a little nap," but the other part said, "You are the only one to protect the dreams of Dad and Lester." The afternoons seemed endless but I never stopped under the tree. Now and then I would doze in the tractor seat and the tractor would veer over and plow through two rows of corn. I would cover up evidence of my negligence by propping up the uprooted plants with loose soil. If two days went by and no one noticed, I knew nature had covered for my carelessness.

When it looked as if the sun was about one hour from dipping below the horizon, I steered the tractor in the direction of the house. There, I would eat supper with the family before climbing onto Lester's tractor, turning on the headlight, and plowing more corn until about 11 p.m. I didn't have a watch, so I headed home when I became too sleepy to avoid uprooting too many rows of corn. By the next morning, Dad and Lester would have managed to refuel the daytime tractor and another day would commence that was identical to the previous one.

This routine continued for about two weeks until Dad and Lester recovered enough to help. I had no idea what to expect in the rest of the world, but it was during those two weeks that I decided to be something—anything—other than a farmer.

HAPPINESS IS FIVE NICKELS IN YOUR OVERALLS

I was seven-years-old when I landed my first job as water boy for the workers in Granddad's hayfields. Even though twenty-five cents a day was a wage that was more than generous, I mustered up the courage to ask Granddad for one extra benefit. "Granddad," I gulped, "I wondered if I could be paid every day—in nickels."

After what seemed like an eternity, he nodded, but the expression on his face and his low grunt told me that I had pushed my luck to the limit and that he would never understand the reason for my request.

I would never be able to explain to him that carrying one quiet quarter in your overalls couldn't compete with five noisy nickels. The jingle of the nickels as I walked or shook my pockets filled me with a sense of newly acquired wealth and security. I couldn't resist boasting about my solvency to my younger sisters. They pretended not to be impressed, but I was delighted to see the thinly veiled envy clouding their eyes.

Occasionally I would weaken and spend one of my nickels for a candy bar and a big Orange Crush at Lone Tree Store, but I was careful never to allow my liquid assets to drop below four nickels. I had adapted to my new image as a high roller and I was no longer willing to walk in overalls that didn't jingle.

When I was nine-years-old and had two summers of experience as a water boy under my belt, I convinced Granddad to promote me to the position of rake operator and pay me two dollars a day, the same wage as the full-grown men received.

The hay rake was a horse-drawn machine with a large iron wheel on either side of a row of curved tines. The tines would collect the hay as the horse pulled the rake across the field. Pressing a foot pedal would cause the row of tines to lift, leaving a neat row of hay to be collected later by a different contraption. Then, the hay would be stacked. After a full day of practice, Granddad reluctantly agreed that I was up to the task.

My new career was launched. I was now in an income bracket that required the use of paper money. In addition to the nickels, each of my pockets now contained a corncob wrapped in dollar bills. The twin bulges in my front pockets announced to the world that I had arrived.

Before long, I had amassed the fourteen dollars necessary to buy the nearly new bicycle at Beasley's hardware store in Linton. I fretted that some other well-to-do person would beat me to it, but in the end, my faith prevailed and the bicycle was mine.

My world then expanded to include miles of gravel road not available to me when I was poor and without transportation. I was now in the fast lane of life but still traveling on gravel roads. I lost a lot of skin learning to ride my bicycle, but the new freedom made all the scrapes worthwhile.

Each year, I continued to learn new skills as I worked for Granddad, but nothing ever measured up to the thrill of my first two jobs when I learned the difference between a quarter and five nickels and felt the security of having a corncob wrapped in dollar bills in each pocket.

HUNTING WITH GRANDDAD: MORE THAN CHASING COONS

I never knew ahead of time when Granddad would take me coon hunting, but sometimes after the milking was finished and supper was over, he and I, accompanied by four howling coonhounds, would head for the woods that lay in back of the farm. Granddad would hold the excited hounds back with one hand while carrying the lantern with the other. I trailed closely behind the swinging light cast by the kerosene lantern.

Once we had found the perfect log upon which to sit in front of our perfect fire, Granddad would stare into the flickering flames and tell me of a world larger than Lone Tree, now and then pausing to tell me what the baying of the hounds meant. To me, it just sounded like all of the dogs barking at once, but Granddad seemed to be able to tell what every hound was doing and thinking. I felt that I was the only kid in the world lucky enough to have a Granddad who could think like a coonhound.

"Old Red just took off after a rabbit, but he'll be back in a minute," he would say, adding, "Leroy and George have treed, but Blacky ain't there yet."

Eventually, all the barking would be coming from one place and off we would go in the direction of the commotion. My job was to climb the tree and shake limbs until the animal fell to the ground. A possum would just fall to the ground and play dead so Granddad would pick it up by the tail and after one sharp blow with a heavy stick, it wasn't just pretending. It would be my job to carry the dead possum around by the tail for the rest of the evening.

If a coon fell out of the tree things were a lot more exciting. They would hit the ground fighting and usually got away from the hounds. They were more trouble to catch but their pelts were worth more. After I cleaned, salted and stretched the pelts, Milt Prichert at the hardware store in Worthington would pay $1.25 for coon hides and.25 cents for possum hides. I don't know why Granddad called it coon hunting when we usually ended up with a possum. There were a lot of things about coon hunting that didn't have anything to do with coons.

THREE SISTERS—ALL GIRLS

Born near the end of 1930, two months before my second birthday, my sister, Elaine, shared some of the family's most trying times. She was very slender with straight, dark hair that my mother cut in a perfect circle around her head, except in the front. All three sisters had the same bowl cut, the only one my mother ever mastered.

When I was very young, I started calling Elaine "Kibby." I think it was the best I could do in my attempt to say "sister."

Store-bought clothes were beyond our means, so Mom made all of Kibby's dresses from flour sacks. Repeated washings would bleach and soften the coarse material, but the "100 lbs. Net" was still visible. My mother would do what she could so the printing on the sack didn't wind up in some embarrassing place on the dress.

Ordinarily, a slender little girl with a bowl haircut wearing a dress made from flour sack would attract curious glances, but it was the middle of the Great Depression, so the only thing that would have warranted attention would have been a well-dressed little girl with a normal hair cut.

For three or four years, until I realized she was a girl, we were the best of buddies. Picking blackberries is one of my most memorable yet painful recollections.

Mom would give each of us a galvanized milk bucket and send us off on our mission. The season was short so we needed to pick every day to have enough to keep us in jams, jellies, and pies through the winter.

After a few hours, we would return home scratched up from battling the prickly blackberry vines, and present our buckets to Mom. Mine would be full but Kibby's would contain only a few berries, and her mouth would be stained a deep purple.

Bonnie was four years younger than I, so my memories of her are not as a playmate so much as a nuisance. She always seemed too young to join in our activities so she trailed along behind Kibby and me.

She was a shy blonde girl for the first two years of her life. By her third year, a little red spot appeared in the center of her blonde hair that expanded until she had an entire mop of hair the color of a copper penny. Her little round face held nothing but tenderness and timidity that kept my parents from ever punishing her. Even when she misbehaved and Dad would approach her with a rolled-up newspaper (which was the way a girl was punished—I got a switch), he would look down at that chubby face with the sagging lower lip as big tears rolled down her round cheeks. Dad could never swat her. He always ended each punishment session with a stern admonishment that he never carried out. "I will let you by this time, but next time you will get a double spanking."

Bonnie displaced me as Kibby's playmate, which was fine with me, considering my disappointment in finding that Kibby wasn't a boy. I was left on my own to find a playmate that would not turn into a girl.

Along came Janet, also not a boy, but not interested in spending time with her sisters. In school she tolerated academics but excelled in sports and music. Her sisters acquired a vocabulary in Latin, but Janet only acquired calluses from catching baseballs. Her first job was as a roller-skating waitress at the Black Swan drive-in restaurant. After her first two nights, she spent all of her tip money on a new Wilson infielder glove, which she slept with for a week. She wanted to appear more feminine, but wearing a nice dress with ruffles wasn't enough when she carried a baseball glove instead of a purse. Her batting average soared, but her relationship with Moose, her boyfriend, sank.

DUDE AND DAISY:
MY BEST FRIENDS

My dog, Dude, stood only about 15 inches tall. He was mostly white except for a black patch that covered one ear. With his white tux and a black top hat cocked jauntily to one side he looked like what Fred Astaire would have looked like if he had been a dog. Thus, his name had to be either Fred or Dude. We chose Dude because it seemed to be a more dog-like title. Also he wagged his tail when he was called Dude, but he responded to Fred with a low growl. I could only wonder about Dude's ancestry. I knew that he couldn't be a Great Dane or a Poodle, but beyond that it was all speculation.

Dude was my constant companion, always bounding along beside me when I left to work in the hay fields. There, he would wait for me under a tree at the edge of the field until I would stop for a drink of water and give him a pat on the head and a portion of the extra sandwich. Even though Dude couldn't speak and ignored my words, he always responded to my feelings well before I told him about them.

Daisy was a sorrel mare with two white stockings on her hind legs and a small white spot on her forehead. In the bright sunlight, her coat was the color of a new copper penny.

In spite of Daisy's beauty, she sometimes did things that can only be described as just plain ornery. She would run to the end of the pasture causing me to chase her for about a quarter of a mile. When she was finally cornered she would stand very still and look at me meekly as if this was just a minor misunderstanding between a very nice horse and a pushy human. She knew other nasty tricks such as expanding her belly while I was attempting to tighten the saddle so that when she breathed out and returned to her normal girth, the saddle would be loose and comfortable. On at least one occasion, Daisy's quest for comfort caused me considerable pain and embarrassment.

When I was ten, I fantasized that the old saddle I purchased for three dollars from Hickey Green was actually trimmed with silver, just like the one used by Roy Rogers. I thought that my horsemanship was right up there with the guys in the movies who wore the white hats and rode horses that could always out run those ridden by the bad guys. Daisy's trick of expanding her belly paid off for her one day as I was showing off my riding ability for my sisters and Dottie Green. Dottie was my friend Hickey's sister and I had a major crush on her, in spite of all of the bad things Hickey told me about her.

On this particular day, Daisy managed to puff out her belly in order to keep the saddle loose. With Dottie watching, I became a little cocky and careless. I did not check the saddle before starting my riding demonstration. One foot was in the stirrup and the other leg was high in the air, mid-swing onto the saddle and Daisy was running down the lane at full speed when the saddle, with me in it, slid under Daisy's belly. After I stopped skidding along the ground, I looked up to see Daisy looking back at me, the empty saddle hanging beneath her belly. I have been told that horses can't smile, but it seemed to me as if Daisy had a big manure-eating grin on her face.

The skin I lost didn't hurt nearly as much as the humiliation of having Dottie see that I was anyone but Roy Rogers. After a reasonable healing period, Dottie still agreed to hold my hand on the school bus. She assured me that, had I been riding Trigger instead of Daisy, I would have looked just like Roy Rogers

MAGIC PLACES

When a summer shower offered a break from the toil in the hay field, I would retreat to my very own private place in the loft of the barn, where I could snuggle into the newly mown hay and let the real world drift away. I would quickly succumb to the magic of the aroma of the hay and the patter of rain on the tin roof as I daydreamed and lost all track of time. I floated above the world on my unguided trek through time and space and visited places unimaginable in Lone Tree.

I saw forest where no two trees were the same shape or color. I saw a desert of multicolored sand with oasis too colorful to be real. In this strange world there were no limits on the shapes, colors, and variations in nature. I never knew how long I had been in my fantasyland when my father would end it all with a call into the barn telling me that the hay field was waiting for me. I would make the abrupt jump back to reality and the field, but the brief time in my magic place would distract me from my tasks for the remainder of the day.

The old swimming hole was another mystical spot. As the creek meandered through the woods behind our house it wound around a large oak tree, creating a pool about twenty feet long with water up to my chest. The roots of the tree had pushed up the ground to create a small green knoll where my dog, Dude, would wait patiently as I frolicked and splashed in my private pool. I would finally exhaust myself and join Dude under the tree to dry and dream. He would give me a look that told me he was smarter than me, but he would tolerate my strange behavior. The leaves of the oak tree broke the sun into thousands of flickering rays of warmth that would carry me away on my magic carpet to places far from Lone Tree. When I was in one of my magic places, my grasp on reality loosened as my mind floated through the universe seeing sights only visible to me. It was then that I knew that heaven had a hayloft and a swimming hole under an oak tree.

THE HAUNTED WALL

Hickey Green and I were lying on our backs under the big maple tree in the yard with nothing more to do than count leaves and complain about having nasty sisters. It was the kind of a lazy summer day that was created just for fishing. We couldn't resist the lure of nature any longer, so we collected our poles and a tin can full of big, juicy fishing worms and headed for the pond in the back of the woods. We were sure that today was the day that one of us would catch the monster catfish that we had convinced each other was lurking in the bottom of the pond.

We settled in our favorite shady spot on the bank and offered our tasty bait to the monster. After hours of being ignored by everything living in the water, we ran out of small talk and surrendered to the peaceful setting. It was one of those times when nothing seemed important enough to disrupt the perfection of the moment. Dude was dozing while Hickey's and my thoughts drifted as aimlessly as the floats on our fishing lines, a time when pondering secrets of the universe seemed like the thing to do.

Hickey finally broke the silence. "You see that old wall up the hill in that clump of oak trees? It's been there forever but we never pay any attention to it. We just walk on by with nary a look. Do you ever wonder how old it really is or what it used to be? Now, it's just a row of mossy old rocks, but once it could have been something real important, like someone's house."

This was the spark needed to ignite the same imaginations that had conjured up the monster catfish. We imagined that, in the distant past, the wall was much taller and surrounding a small log cabin with smoke curling out from a crude stone chimney. We each offered a guess as to how many squirrels had scurried along its top and where rabbits snuggled beside it to escape the fury of a blizzard. We were sure that no passing bear could resist the temptation to scratch his back on the wall. We wondered if a family once lived there and did they have children. Did the children survive this harsh life long enough to grow up and, if so, where were they now? We agreed that since the wall couldn't talk, its secrets were locked away forever. Resigned to the fact that our questions could never be answered, we collected our fishing gear and silently followed Dude back home.

Thoughts about the wall haunted me for the next week. I couldn't seem to get back to thinking about baseball or the new girl in school. I knew I had to visit the wall and try to sort out truth from fantasy. Sunday afternoon Dude and I were on our way back through the woods. This time I didn't bother trying to catch a fish but went directly to the wall and found a shady spot where I could lean back and have deep thoughts.

I closed my eyes, and started thinking of baseball and the new girl in school. Would I ever really pitch for the

Saint Louis Cardinals and would Dorothy Hostetler ever sit by me on the school bus? My pleasant daydreams were soon invaded by a parade of strange sounds and images that I couldn't understand nor could I stop.

There were shadowy silhouettes walking among teepees speaking a language that I couldn't understand. I heard shots from guns that I could not see. I was surrounded by covered wagons, riders on horseback, and small groups of people hurrying through the forest but making no sound. I felt the presence of large animals so close that I could feel their breath pulsating against my cheek, yet they were invisible. The sounds from a small cabin of children laughing, the sounds of deer bounding through dry leaves, and squirrels dropping nuts from trees echoed through my mind. Maybe the old wall was finally giving up the secrets that it had kept for centuries. Maybe it was waiting for someone to ask.

DODGE CITY UNDER THE OAK TREE

Jack and Gene Hawkins lived a half mile down the road on the next farm. Jack was a year older than Gene and I. We were buddies and did all the things that boys between the ages of seven and nine do such as making a lot of noise and pretending to be grown-up cowboys. We imagined that we could do anything Gene Autry and Roy Rogers could do, except our horses were even smarter and we were faster on the draw. We looked forward to watching our favorite cowboy heroes chase and beat up on a bunch of bad guys in the Saturday night movies, but we needed a little more action to fill in the rest of the week.

The Dodge City of our fantasy world was beneath a huge oak tree behind the barn on the Hawkins farm. Grass didn't grow in this shady spot and the soil was soft fine clay. The ends of corncobs were ideal tools to form furrows in the soft clay, the streets of Dodge. Each of us chose our favorite corncobs that would be the main characters in our western dramas. They all had names and personalities, but only the most attractive ones could become heroes. A few of the less colorful cobs were kept in a separate pile to be used as part-time characters such as the sheriff or the undertaker. Any of us could borrow from this pile to add to the cast in our dramas.

The action started slowly but quickly progressed into furious conflicts as our corncobs took on lives of their own. We had it all—gun battles, fist fights, and long chases on horseback. We were a part of exciting adventures that were completely beyond our control. Sometimes the action became so fierce that the streets of Dodge were leveled and a break in the action was required to allow time to rebuild.

Only much later did a deep thinker tell me that our corncobs and we were one. It hurt a little at first to hear that your ego could be contained in a single corncob, but, with time, this revelation didn't seem to detract from these magical times under the big oak tree with corncobs and loose dirt.

ASSAULT ON THE SENSES

There were plenty of things on the farm that did not delight the senses. The most aggressive assault on our sense of smell occurred in the barn in late April every year. During the winter, the horses and cows spent a great deal of time in their stalls where they relieved themselves freely for months on end. Layers of straw were added to combat this onslaught, causing the floor of the barn to rise accordingly. By early spring, the ceiling barely cleared my head and my dad had to enter the barn in a stooped position.

Each spring we were faced with the task of lowering the floor to its original level. With our eyes watering, Dad and I would rake out the reeking mixture and load it into a contraption called a manure spreader. The manure spreader was a large wagon equipped with a screw-like mechanism on the back, which hurled the manure high into the air in all directions as the horses pulled it through the cornfield. My father always seemed to discuss politics during this chore.

I also remember the big blizzard at a time I could have done without. The morning seemed to be the start of a typical dreary winter day, but by early afternoon a gray sky and a cold damp wind appeared as reliable omens that a storm was on its way. The animals sensed well before the people that Lone Tree was facing more that a mild change in the weather. The four horses were huddled behind the barn with their backs to the wind, their heads lowered, and their eyes closed. The cows assumed similar postures only a few feet away from the horses. Only the hogs seemed to be completely oblivious to the portents of danger.

The blizzard of the decade arrived with a fury during the night. We awoke to a strange world of white with drifts as high as the tops of the fences. Since our familiar territory had been changed to an alien landscape, digging a path to the barn was hard work, but also a great adventure. The cows did not share our excitement. We were an hour late arriving at the barn and the tone of their moos told me that they were in a testy mood from being cold, hungry, and carrying an overload of milk around in an uncomfortable place. After all the animals were fed I started my milking chores with the cows that seemed to be in the most pain, although when they have aching udders, even gentle cows will not tolerate cold hands. To make my hands acceptable to these picky cows, I would place them palm to palm between the cow's udder and the inside of her leg. This was the only warm place on the cow that I could reach from my milking stool. When my hands were warmer the cow would usually allow me to end her suffering, and her body English would let me know that she was feeling better and would soon return to her comfortable role as a contented cow.

The three cats living in the barn gathered about ten feet away in anticipation of the stream of warm milk that I would send arching in their direction. The horses and cows spent the remainder of the day in the barn, and the hogs lolled in a disorderly pile under their shed still unconcerned with the weather.

MY TWELFTH BIRTHDAY:
YOUNG DANIEL BOONE

My twelfth birthday, February 22, 1941, was coming up and for months I had been dreaming of having my very own 22-caliber rifle and a hunting knife—the only things preventing me from becoming the most famous rabbit and squirrel hunter in Lone Tree. I was asking for a lot for just one birthday, so I made a deal with my Dad that I would sell enough walnuts, possum hides, and hickory nuts to cover half of the cost of my expensive gifts.

The rifle cost $16.95 and the knife $3.50, so it took quite a while to amass the necessary cash, but when I sold a peck of walnuts to Homer Kemp for two dollars, I had it all in my cigar box three days before my birthday. Homer didn't need that many walnuts, but he wanted to help with my quest to become a famous hunter.

After what seemed like eons, my birthday finally arrived and I had my two presents. I felt a foot taller with my rifle on my shoulder and my knife in its scabbard, strapped around my waist. Homer now referred to me as Lone Tree's very own home-grown Daniel Boone. During the week after my birthday, I slept with the rifle beside my bed and my knife under the pillow. For several days, I didn't fire the gun for fear of wearing it out.

I quickly forgot all of the trials and tribulations of life on the farm and instead focused on the larger responsibilities that came with being the Daniel Boone of Lone Tree. I used my last coon skin to make a hat just like the one Daniel Boone wore in the movie. It was black and white on top with a long tail that would swing behind my head when I walked. I practiced walking through the woods without making a sound. Just like the other Daniel Boone, I could hear every acorn that dropped from a tree and the slightest sounds from dry leaves being disturbed. Dude and I would spend all my free time roaming the woods. Our harvest of game was limited to an occasional rabbit or squirrel which I would roast over a fire and share with Dude, but I was happy. Being twelve years old, being with Dude and having my own gun and hunting knife was a good life. I wondered if the real Daniel Boone ever felt as free and at peace with the world as I felt walking through the woods behind our farm.

PRAIRIE COLLEGE:
NOT A REAL COLLEGE

I don't know where Prairie College got its name because it wasn't a college, or even a high school, but only a small elementary school in Lone Tree with never more than a total of thirty students in all eight grades. It was a one-room, rectangular building with a belfry on the top and thirty desks surrounding a potbellied stove on the inside .The teacher's desk was on a raised platform at the front of the room directly in front of a long recitation bench. In front of the school was a well with a hand pump and two paths paved with cinders curved around each side of the school on their way to the outhouses, each with its custom-built shelf for the Sears Catalog.

. My only classmates in the fifth grade were the Hayes twins, Leland and Liebert. In March, the twins had their sixteenth birthday so, as was the custom, they returned to the farm and we never saw them again at school after we celebrated their "coming-of-age" with a small party in the classroom. With the twins gone, there was no one to be in the sixth grade with me. The teacher, Harry Fiscus, deemed that I needed classmates more than I needed the sixth grade, so I received a double promotion and went to the seventh grade where I would have two classmates. It wasn't a big deal because in the one-room school, I had already heard the material at least five times.

Mr. Fiscus was a tall man with black, almost fuzzy hair that he oiled down every morning with Brilliantine. But by mid afternoon, little clumps would start to break loose. We referred to them as Mr. Fiscus's horns and we spent a lot of time speculating as to when they would spring up. He also stuttered when he was excited, so some of the older kids did nasty things just to hear him.

Mr. Fiscus had two suits. On Mondays, Wednesdays and Fridays, he would wear the striped suit and on the other two days, he would wear the brown one. It must have been difficult to arrange to clean the suits because by mid-semester, the collars would become dark and slick from the hair oil he used to try to control his unruly locks. Once the collars became saturated, they seemed to not get any worse for the rest of the year. He would start the process over again each fall with an oil-free collar.

Mr. Fiscus was a good teacher. He was smart enough to teach us new things and big enough to beat up on the seventh and eighth graders whenever it was necessary. On one occasion, he beat up on Chancey Green, and then tossed him in a ditch in front of the school. He stuttered a lot that day.

Chancey's little brother, Hickey, took Chancey home after the incident. The next day, their father, Leonard, showed up at school to shake Harry's hand and congratulate him on finally getting Chancey's attention.

THE FUNERAL
FOR GREASY HELMS

Of the twenty-eight students who attended
Prairie College Elementary School, three were from
the Helms family. They belonged to a religious sect
that did not permit them to join in celebrations of
holidays, birthdays, or recite the Pledge of Allegiance
to the flag, which was a part of the normal routine
for starting the school day. Every morning had
an awkward beginning as we recited the Pledge of
Allegiance while the Helms children stood, silently
staring at the floor.

Helen, the oldest of the Helms children, a tall and
very shy girl, seemed to have accepted a fate of standing
alone watching other people with joy in their lives that
she could never know. Her family found wastefulness as
distasteful as vanity, which may have been why Helen
didn't waste a lot of soap washing her long brown hair.
As a result, it appeared very oily and unkempt, earning
her the nickname of "Greasy."

The cruel title stuck and everyone joined in the new
game of chanting, "Greasy Helms, Greasy Helms."

One Monday morning, Greasy didn't show up for
school. Her brothers reported that she had something
really bad called typhoid fever. Her family believed that
their fervent prayers would cure her and medicine was

not necessary, so Greasy's recovery depended entirely on the magical properties of prayer and sassafras tea. She died the next week.

The shy girl that we had treated so cruelly was gone forever and no one had the opportunity to say, "I didn't mean it." "Greasy" became "Helen" the moment Mr. Fiscus announced her death. The climate in school became very somber as we all tried to justify our bad behavior. Little did we know that our penance was yet to be paid.

Helen's mother asked Mr. Fiscus to select six students to act as pallbearers. In spite of my fierce, silent pleas, I was one of the chosen six. We were miserable as we considered carrying the target of our sins to her grave. The only dead person I had ever seen was my grandmother, and at the time, I was too young to grasp that she wouldn't be around to serve me buttermilk and biscuits the next morning.

On the morning of the funeral we six, all in our best clothes, were lined up in the front pew waiting to perform our dreaded duty as pallbearers, but we felt as if we were six sinners sitting in front of Helen's coffin waiting to enter the gates of hell.

We all recalled Homer Allcock's sermons, and we knew we were guilty of every sin he mentioned, especially the part about loving your neighbor. We looked away and tried to imagine that we were somewhere else far away as we carried Helen the thirty feet that seemed to be a mile for the five minutes that would seem to never end.

We mumbled silly things to each other as doubts and fear flooded our minds. Could Helen know how sorry we felt for the way we treated her? Was she different now and maybe didn't need to hear of our regrets? But did she realize that we needed to tell her anyway? If only we could talk to her one time we could tell her how sorry we were, and maybe also ask her what heaven was like. Was it worth being good all the time? Did bad things like getting sick or skinning you knee ever happen there? If there were only good things in heaven, were some better than others? Would Helen be amused at our vain attempt to deal with our guilt, or would she be sorry that she could not share her newly found peace and happiness with us?

Willie Cox said, "She's probably sittin' on a cloud clappin' and laughin' while we're totin' her around."

I was sure Willie was wrong because if Helen was enjoying our misery she couldn't be in heaven and none of us would get there either.

The lowering of Helen into her final resting place didn't ease our pain as much as we had hoped. The name Greasy would never be uttered again, but we would never forget Helen.

THE WRITTEN WORD

During the 1930s, the media in Lone Tree was limited to the weekly edition of the *Linton Lantern* and the radio. The nearest library was six miles away in Linton, so even with a large daily dose of juicy rumors, people's appetite for entertainment went largely unsatisfied.

My cousin Beaner Clemens's house had a special place just for books but our house didn't have such a place, nor a need for one. Reading was not a high priority in my family. Dad decreed: "Nothing in them there books makes you a better farmer or gives you more energy for plowing more ground or pitching more hay."

During the summers my reading was limited to cowboy stories in the magazines that were passed around by farmers working in the hayfields. These publications cost fifteen cents new, but I never laid eyes on a new one. The books spent most of their lives protruding from the pockets of men's overalls, where they were handy for a few minutes of diversion under a shade tree at lunch time.

The books would be circulated among interested farmers until the accumulation of dirt and sweat made the print unreadable. The books would then be retired to the outhouse to spend their remaining days next to the Sears catalog, waiting to depart the reading world one page at a time. My interest in these limp little paperbacks was waning, so I was not terribly sad when they disappeared from the hayfield to spend their final days in the outhouse.

These paperbacks didn't interest me much because all of the characters in the stories seemed to lead such similar lives. The hero on the white horse always seemed to be able to overtake the bad guy on the dull brown horse with the lighter saddle.

After knocking the villain off of his horse and giving him a thorough thrashing, the hero would calmly retrieve his white hat, place it over his unruffled hair and ride his prancing steed off into a perfect sunset. I grew weary of the same old story in which only the names of the cowboy and the horse changed. I was also disappointed that the cowboy always seemed to have a wonderful, close relationship with his horse, but he never knew the right thing to say to the local schoolmarm.

It was not until I entered the eighth grade that I discovered that there were a lot of other books out there besides these tattered magazines and Dad's copy of Zane Grey's *Robber's Roost*.

I was the only student to survive all the way to the eighth grade so the teacher, Mr. Fiscus, decided it was not worth his time to teach a class for only one student. Instead, I was given a book each week to keep me entertained while the classes composed of more than one student recited on the long bench in front of the room. I was lucky. I could daydream or read my book with no obligation to listen to anything going on anywhere else in the room. Of course, I always had the option to pay attention if anything interesting happened up front.

The new world inside of books was filled with people doing things I had never been able to squeeze into my life. I became acquainted with Tom Sawyer, Huckleberry Finn, and Daniel Boone. I shared all of their adventures. I helped Tom paint the fence with Becky. I hunted "bars" with Daniel Boone. I had discovered a bigger and better place, and I knew I would never be willing to abandon my new friends who lived in the pages of the books I had read.

After a few weeks, my appetite for new adventures grew more voracious than Mr. Fiscus's ability to supply them, so I looked for new sources of books. My hunt led me to Cousin Beaner's house where a shelf full of books sat, waiting to be opened. Beaner offered to lend me one book at a time if he could keep my pocketknife as collateral. I didn't think this was entirely fair, but I decided to accept one unfair thing in my life and hope that when the next one came along I might come out on the winning side.

With basketball practice and a long bus ride, I had less time to read during high school, but I didn't miss it too much because the adventures from my English book paled in comparison to my old heroes. I just couldn't scare up much concern for what happened to Ivanhoe or the Lady in the Lake.

THE BARN DANCE

I was ten-years-old and had never even seen a barn dance. It was hard to understand how we could have so many barns around but not a single dance ever happened in any of them. All I knew about them I learned from listening to the radio station in Nashville where they described the hoedowns at the *Grand Ole Opry*. There was at least one fiddler, and some other musicians and a lot of people dancing. I wanted to see a real live one.

Finally my wish was coming true. Granddad said that we were going to have our very own barn dance right here in Lone Tree. He explained that people had the idea years ago, but not until now were they able to get everything that was needed together on a single night. Freddie Funkhouser's barn with the wood floor was empty and the only two local musicians, Waldo Gross on the fiddle, and Curley Callihan with his banjo, agreed to furnish the music. I had already heard them play at a box supper. Waldo was pretty good, but Curley could have used a few lessons on his banjo.

Millie Pankey, the telephone operator, spent the whole week breaking into party line gossip with the announcement of the big event.

I wanted to see what happened at a real barn dance. Would people dress up in their Sunday clothes and did enough people know how to dance to make it worthwhile? Granddad thought it would be a nice quiet affair with the preacher, Homer Allcock, there to keep the devil on the outside, but I was sure some of the local folks would get excited and misbehave. Liquor was not allowed, but everyone knew that the Truitt brothers would have a jug of hard cider stashed behind the barn for those who needed a little nip to jack up their courage. I didn't dare tell Dad, but I hoped the Truitt brothers would show up. I wanted to see how grown ups acted after they were overloaded with hard cider. I knew that Dad and Uncle John were pretty funny, but how would people act that had a head start on being funny?

The big night arrived with my sisters and I and five other curious kids coming early and finding a perch in the loft where we could dangle our legs over the edge and look directly down on the big event about to occur on the floor below. We didn't know what was going to happen but we couldn't wait for it to start. We all held our hands over our ears while Curley and Waldo tuned their instruments, but after they finished it still didn't sound like they were playing the same tune. Billy Blevins said he had heard real dance music on the radio and it didn't sound much like the noises Curly and Waldo were making. It didn't seem to matter to the four or five couples on the floor doing their version of dancing.

Maude and Orval Miller had told Millie they wouldn't be there, but there they were among the very first to be peering in the door before going in. Maude was a real showstopper in her bright purple dress and pink hat, but Orval didn't seem to have taken the dance that seriously. He was dressed about right for milking but a little too casual for a dance. Maude was embarrassed and giggly as she pulled Orval toward the dance floor. They made a funny sight but not very different from the other dancers. We were watching our grown up neighbors move parts of their body that we had never noticed before. Maybe this was a place where grown ups were supposed to act like kids and kids were supposed to act like grown ups. Cousin Junior Bays said maybe having the kids there watching was ruining the fun for the adults, and we should not be sitting above them watching, but we should be behind the barn looking through a knot hole in the wall.

My sister, Kibby, spent the evening in the back of the loft peeping through a crack counting the trips to the jug that everyone made. She said some of the men, including Curley and Waldo, were spending a lot of time there. Maude was encouraging Orval to loosen up and relax but after a few trips to the jug he was having a lot of trouble standing up, let alone dancing, so she guided him out of the barn and took him home early.

I was embarrassed when the kids told me that my dad and mom were just as funny as the others, but after watching them for a while I had to agree. Mom seemed to have done it before, but Dad acted like he was pumping water from the well. By that time others were getting into the swing of things, so Maude and Orval were barely missed. Russell Potter drifted away from his wife Beulah and was in the middle of the floor shaking just like our old rooster just before he died. After Silas Jones did his elephant walk, he started dancing way too close to the Widow Swaby. His wife, Delphi interrupted the second dance by having a snit that caused the Widow Swaby to run from the dance floor and Silas to follow Delphi out of the barn. From our perch in the loft we could not hear what Delphi said but it must have been really bad because everyone, including Curley and Waldo, stopped to listen.

Except for Thadius Spice, the teenagers were good dancers. Bennie Fiscus and Kate Pankey were the best. Bennie danced a lot like Fred Astaire, but he didn't clean up as well. The teenagers would slip out of the barn, too, but they didn't go to the jug.

By 11:30, the preacher was sleepy, the jug was empty and Curley and Waldo had used up all of their tunes, so the one and only Lone Tree Barn Dance was winding down. We in the hayloft had seen enough strange sights for one evening.

I was sure that Silas and Ollie, considering the way they acted up at the barn dance, would not show up Sunday morning in church, but when the bell in the belfry rang, there they both were sitting at opposite ends of the back pew. Homer had eyes like an eagle when it came to spotting sinners. He was glaring at Silas and Ollie. We couldn't wait to hear Homer describe the details of their quick trip to hell. Silas and Ollie had acted really silly and a little drunk at the dance, but today I felt sorry for them as they sat alone in the back pew with their heads bowed while Homer gave the his best ever description of the hell and damnation they were doomed to face. He made it sound as if they were never even going to get close enough to the pearly gates to be turned away. He didn't announce the names of the week's biggest sinners, but he gave them his best stare of disgust during all the scariest parts of his sermon. It was a good day for most people because Homer devoted his entire sermon to saving the souls of Silas and Ollie and everyone else got a free pass.

BOX SUPPERS
AND COURTING

Maude Miller was the self appointed matchmaker in Lone Tree. Her own love life had not satisfied her teenage fantasies. She confided to her friend, Panzy, that with better guidance during her courting days she could have done better than Orval, her disgruntled husband of twenty-five years. She was dedicated to her mission of providing young folks with the help that she had not received before she settled for Orval. To her, any young person with a sad look of longing or even a slight tinge of lust in their eyes was a potential lost soul, doomed to live an unfulfilling life if she didn't come to their rescue.

Maude was convinced that box suppers were the perfect settings, next to heaven, for ideal matches to be made. When Maude deemed them necessary, they were held on Friday nights at the picnic area in back of Providence Baptist church. Young women would bring samples of their best cooking in a box all wrapped and tied with fancy ribbons to be auctioned off to young men with good appetites, money, and honorable intentions. Along with the meal, the high bidder would have the pleasure of the young lady's company during the consumption of the contents of the box. There would be adults at nearby tables, eavesdropping and monitoring the young lady's demeanor and the young man's table manners.

It was a time when the girls could show off their best recipes and nicest clothes and the boys would take a bath, wear clean clothes and try to appear dapper. Parents would bring their own food, sit on the sidelines and quietly watch for signs that this good food and beautiful setting was helping to ignite a tiny flame of love for their chosen couple.

There was always a lot of drama and tension at the events and they seldom turned out according to Maude's plan. One Friday night in September of 1940 was no exception.

It was a beautiful fall evening and Maude was radiant with optimism. All the box suppers, with their brightly colored ribbons, were neatly arranged on a picnic table in front of the audience of about twenty people sitting on folding chairs. It was Maude's time to realize her calling and make her mark as the matchmaker of Lone Tree.

Melvin Finley had a strong hankering to become better acquainted with Allie Pines but, so far his contact with her was limited to a wave and a broad grin as he drove the tractor past her house on his way to the cornfield. He enjoyed it, but he yearned for a closer relationship, maybe one where they could hold hands and talk about silly things. Melvin was seventeen and a good farmer, but his time in the cornfield had not been much help in developing his social skills. Maude told him that he was doomed to have a love life consisting of only looking and yearning if he didn't get some help. His hope was that the box supper would spice up his relationship with Allie.

Allie's parents were aware of Melvin's attention to their daughter but they preferred a match with Leon Gilbert. Like Melvin, he wasn't Clark Gable, but he was less bashful and his folks had a larger farm, although Melvin was acceptable as a backup plan. Allie's mom told her that she was already seventeen, had two boys interested in her and time was a wastin'. If she waited another year, pickin's for a beau could get purty thin.

The bidding commenced and the first few boxes went mainly to steady daters. Everyone knew the excitement of the auction would be the competition for Allie's box supper and her company for the evening. The bidding rapidly reached sixty cents as Melvin and Leon topped the others offers. Melvin was getting worried and nervously counting his money. He only had seventy-five cents and he knew Leon had almost a dollar. His only hope was that Allie and her box would not be worth seventy-five cents to Leon. His concerns changed when a third bidder joined in the auction. Jake Pritchert raised a whole dime up to seventy cents. Melvin shot his whole wad by raising a nickel while Leon remained silent. Jake won the company of Allie and the honor of sharing her fried chicken and gooseberry pie for eighty cents.

Events went down hill for the remainder of the evening. Melvin shared supper with Clemintine Baughman, his third choice, and Leon dined with his sister for only forty cents. The evening was tense as girls shared their box supper with the highest bidder while glaring at a preferred partner at another table.

Maude was distraught—nothing had turned out as

she had hoped. However, she was devout to her calling and could not leave young romance in Lone Tree to drift aimlessly for very long. She would have to schedule another box supper right away to set everything right. This time, she would either not invite Jake or loan Leon some bidding cash.

SATURDAY NIGHT-BATHS, MOVIES AND HAMBURGERS

Saturday was the day we finished our chores early so we could take our baths, dress in clean clothes, and head out for a big night in Linton with a western at the Cine movie theater followed by a hamburger and a Coca Cola at the Green Parrot Cafe.

I dreaded the bath in the round galvanized tub on the back porch, but Mom would not let us leave the house until we were bathed and she had checked us over for dirty spots, particularly behind our ears. Seeing us all spiffed up on Saturday night might help people forget what we looked like the rest of the week, she often said.

I was the oldest and often the dirtiest, but somehow I was always fourth in line for the tub after my sisters. I wouldn't have minded being fourth in line if I could have had my own bath water, but there was only enough water for two tubs: one for the adults and one for the kids. I often wondered how old I needed to be to have my own bath water and why I needed to wash all over for just a few dirty spots.

After scrubbing myself in the gray, lukewarm water with lye soap, I would put on a pair of clean overalls and join the family in the six mile trip to Linton in our Model A Ford. We would hope to see a movie starring

Gene Autry, Hopalong Cassidy or one of our other heroes chasing outlaws through the mountains, but sometimes we would have to sit through a boring movie with not one single horse.

When I felt really brave, I would sit in the front row at the movies with Lolly Clayton. I liked Lolly and I thought I might ask if I could hold hands with her when the theater was dark. But I decided that if I did, she might expect me to pay for her hamburger and Coca Cola. Granddad had warned me about fast women and, for all I knew, Lolly could be one.

I knew it would be safe to play checkers with her, but holding hands seemed too risky. Even if she cheated at checkers, it wouldn't cost me any money. Nevertheless, I would spend the entire trip home regretting my decision not to ask to hold Lolly's hand when the theater was dark.

THE KEEPER OF THE PEACE

Most folks in most small towns worried about their community growing too fast or too slowly, but those who lived in Worthington, four miles east of Lone Tree, took great pride in the fact that its population had not changed for three decades. The number hovered around 1500 if a few cows and chickens were included in the head count. It was a quiet town where no one locked their doors, and the back entrance to Willy Barnes's feed store remained open all night, guarded only by an overfed but ill-tempered rooster.

Folks in Worthington thought it was nice that everybody who wanted to live in Worthington seemed to already be there, including Tully Conway, Worthington's self-appointed sheriff. He was not the only person in town doing things that were hard to explain to strangers, but he was one that you could not help but notice. If one were to ask Tully why the town was so peaceful, he would take all of the credit. Only the real sheriff might disagree. Folks with minds that were out of kilter were tolerated and even enjoyed as long as they made the community more interesting and weren't too nasty toward people or farm animals.

Tully was a slight man with a large drooping mustache and one eye that seemed slow to focus. He seldom removed his battered brown cowboy hat, but his sister, Grendel, let it be known that there was nothing under his hat worth seeing anyway.

Anchored with a piece of rawhide, the holster bearing his rusty old gun appeared very large for his skinny leg. His entire ego seemed to be packed into the shiny badge he wore on his chest. Even though Worthington had a part-time sheriff, Tully considered himself the only real sheriff and the only law officer capable of protecting local folks during those times when major crimes were likely to occur.

Tully figured that time was Saturday night, what with everybody's weekly grocery money in their pockets. The time was ripe for criminals to strike. He knew that the big-time operators like John Dillinger and Bonnie and Clyde would not bother unless grocery money was in town.

By early evening on any given Saturday, Tully would have treated himself to at least three beers and have settled into the spare chair in Virgil White's barbershop, where he planned his strategy for protecting the town that evening. He considered himself the equal of any criminal who would dare venture inside the city limits of Worthington on a Saturday night.

Tully rendered himself invisible by pulling his old hat down over his eyes, as he prowled the streets in search of suspicious characters on the verge of committing serious crime. He never came up empty-handed. There was always someone out there who was a serious threat. As soon as they were spotted, Tully would make a daring arrest and march the dangerous criminals down Main Street to the jail. Billy, the real sheriff, would thank Tully for the fine police work and take charge of the prisoners

As soon as Tully was out of sight, Billy would release the prisoner—usually after a friendly exchange about the weather. I don't know what would have happened if Tully had ever arrested somebody who wasn't willing to play their part in the drama.

ALFIE DILLARD'S DREAM TO BECOME WORLDLY

During the early 1940s, World War II was raging and several of the young men around Lone Tree were being drafted to serve in the army. Most of them could have qualified for a deferment to stay and farm, but few chose that option. It just wasn't the right thing to do in Lone Tree in those times.

Alfie Dillard was nineteen-years-old and had never been away from home further than Indianapolis and he wanted to see more of the world, especially the ocean. He dreamed of a day when he could wade in it and feel the sand between his toes. He made the big decision to enlist in the Navy before he could be drafted into the Army. It could be his only chance to satisfy his lifelong dream of seeing the world and the ocean. His folks wanted him to help with the farm as long as possible, but he had made up his mind.

The Navy accepted Alfie and within a month he was on his way to San Diego. In three months, he had survived basic training and arrived back in Lone Tree for two weeks of shore leave before reporting for duty. The local folks couldn't wait to see if three months in a foreign place, living with strangers, and seeing the ocean had changed him.

Millie, the local telephone operator, helped to spread the word that Alfie would show up at Gibson's Drug Store on his first evening home. Fifteen people were already there when he came strutting in wearing his white Navy uniform with the big square collar and announced that he had seen one side of the ocean and he was already feeling pretty worldly. He said that the ocean was even better than he had imagined and he couldn't wait to be in the middle of it on a ship.

Folks seemed to be most interested when he told of his weekend pass in San Diego with two of his buddies from Kansas. Alfie said, "It was a real big town full of people not paying any attention to one another but, after a lot of walking, we finally found one street where a lot of friendly people, mostly girls, were just taking nice walks. They were really pretty, but they dressed a lot fancier than any girls I had ever seen before. They had on high heeled shoes that caused them to walk kinda wobbly, real big hair, and skirts that they had outgrown about two years ago.

One of the pretty ones walked right up to me and said, 'Hi, Sailor. What's your name?' I wanted to be friendly and act real smart, too, so I said, 'I'm Alfie Dillard from Lone Tree and what did your Mama name you?' She said her name was Fannie, then, right out of the blue, she asked me if I wanted to have a good time. I thought she must be real patriotic to be so friendly to a sailor from out of town. Maybe she used to work for the USO. I didn't want her to think that I had fallen off the back of the hay wagon so, quick as a wink, I said, 'I am on a three-day pass from the base and, sure, I want to have a good time.' Then she said, 'Would you like to go somewhere and do something fun?" I said, 'You bet I would. How about a movie?' She said, 'I like movies but that would take two hours. Can you afford it?' Right then I realized that the poor little thing didn't have much money and she was worried about me spending all of mine so I told her, 'You don't need to worry about that. I got paid for the whole month and I will pay treat you to a movie and even buy you a hamburger and Coke float after the show.'

Either she didn't like hamburgers or I said something that hurt her feelings, because all of a sudden she started staring at me with the strangest look on her face like she didn't understand what I was saying, or maybe couldn't hear me. She didn't seem as friendly then, but I think she still liked me a little because as she walked away she turned and said that I should save my money and the Navy was sure lucky to have guys like me protecting the country."

COTTON TUTTLE: THE IMPORTANCE OF GOOD MANNERS

Cotton was Willy and Midge Tuttle's only son. He was a big twelve-year-old with a mop of curly blonde hair and wide set eyes that always seemed to be asking "Where am I?" His parents wanted their only son to be perfect, but in spite of their best efforts, he came up a little short of average, even on a good day. Willy was teaching him how to be a good farmer while Midge spent a lot of time adjusting the straps on his overalls, but she was mainly interested in his learning proper table manners so he wouldn't attract so much attention at ice cream socials and other events where a lot of eating took place.

Every evening before supper Midge would go over the list of important dos and don'ts with Cotton:

"Always accept invitations to eat because if you don't people will think you don't like their cookin'."

"The polite thing to say when you get an invitation is always 'Yes, Ma'am, that would be really nice.'"

"You don't blow on your soup no matter how hot it is."

"You pretend that you like everything on the table, but don't be greedy. Two helpin's are enough of anything, especially apple pie."

"You don't talk about anything that might upset people until everyone is finished eatin' and pushed back from the table."

Cotton had it all memorized and was sure he was ready for any social occasion that might pop up.

Willy wasn't having as much success teaching Cotton to be a good farmer. A major problem occurred when Willy was sitting on top of a load of hay while instructing Cotton on how to drive the tractor. Cotton was so excited with his new responsibilities that he rounded a curve a little too fast and dumped the load of hay with Willy under it in the ditch. Willy was pinned under the hay with only his head showing. He called for Cotton to go down the road to the Beasley farm and get help. Cotton said, "Yes sir, " and went running down the road as fast as he could go.

Fanny Beasley answered the door with her usual sickly sweet smile and said, "Hello, Cotton Boy, we ain't seen you in quite a spell. We was just sittin' down to breakfast but there is plenty for everyone so sit and have a bite with us." Cotton remembered his mom's words and replied, "Yes, Ma'am, that would be really nice."

After a big breakfast of pork chops, fried eggs, and biscuits, Lorne Beasley, the last to push back from the table said, "Cotton, how is your pa these days?" Cotton saw that everyone was finished eating so he knew it would be all right to tell him about Pa's fix. "Pa ain't too good. He is back down the road a piece under a load of hay". Lorne jumped up and said "Shucks Cotton, why didn't you say something. Let's get on down there and dig him out." When they reached the front gate they saw Willy coming down the road jumping up and down and yelling, but still too far away for them to hear what he was saying. Cotton knew his Pa was acting like that because he was so happy to be out from under the hay. Cotton could hardly wait to tell his Ma how polite he had been.

THE PREACHER:
A GOOD REASON NOT TO SIN

Our parents thought we should do a little praying before going to bed, but they didn't check on us and most of the time we forgot to do it. The serious praying took place Sunday mornings at Providence Baptist Church.

All the local families would gather promptly at 10:30 each Sunday morning before the formal services started for a short period of visiting and discussing the weather, including a little talk about what the Farmer's Almanac predicted for the remainder of the growing season.

While the grownups visited, the kids would play in the yard behind the church until the gong of the big bell in the belfry reminded them that it was time to go inside and learn how to be good. The mothers would stare daggers at the kids as they stormed into the church with their best clothes stained from the wet grass, but the real punishment would come later at home.

Homer Allcock was the only preacher I had ever known, so to me he looked exactly like a preacher should look. He was a tall man with less hair than he needed and a beak-like nose that dipped sharply at the end. The front of his head was bare but there was a large lump of mud-brown hair near the back. Homer seemed to have left the care of this tuft to God, who evidently didn't consider it very important. His undersized mouth seemed to be frozen in a puckered mode, giving the impression that there was no way it could be used to conjure up a smile. Disdain and disgust were his best expressions.

The pant legs of his brown suit never quite reached the white socks he wore with his black Oxfords. Old timers who remembered when his brown preacher's suit was new recalled a time when his pants fit, but too many trips to the creek to baptize folks had caused some shrinkage over the years.

No special education was required to be a preacher. One had only to hear "the callin" directly from God and need the extra money. According to Granddad, Homer did have two qualifications that made him acceptable as a man of the cloth. He was a very bad farmer, which afforded him the spare time he needed to be a preacher, and he wore glasses, which made him appear smart enough for the job.

Homer's sermons consisted mostly of quotes from the Bible and his own interpretations of their real meaning. After doing all he could to lay a well-deserved guilt trip on the congregation, Homer would offer a prayer about financial obligations to God and then ask that the offering plate be passed around. It would be passed around by two of the kids with shiny faces and grass stains on their white shirts or blouses.

Homer's sermon was punctuated with various hymns that we would all stand and sing, such as *The Old Rugged Cross* and *Onward Marching Christian Soldiers*. I still remember the farmers' big, rough, callused hands holding a worn, dull red songbook down far enough so that the kids could see it.

After the service, all would file out, shaking the hand of the preacher. Those who needed to offered a detailed excuse for having missed church the previous Sunday. They had spent the entire service thinking one up so they were usually pretty good.

LEARNING ABOUT GOD

During the many Sunday mornings that I spent squeezed between my parents in the pews at the Providence Baptist Church, I developed my own sense of religion. In spite of trying to pass the time by daydreaming about baseball or trying to trick my sisters into laughing out loud in church, sometimes I would get so bored that I would actually try to listen to Homer's sermon. He talked a lot about someone named God as if He were right there in the church with us; however, neither my sisters nor I ever spotted Him.

Homer also said that God had a kid named Jesus who was always getting into trouble, especially with the Romans. I thought the wise choice was to pay attention to the Dad.

God was not easy to understand. Homer said he was very powerful and could do anything he wanted, but he never explained why he couldn't keep his own kid in line or why so many bad things happened when he was in the neighborhood

Homer talked too loud, but he was our preacher and was supposed to know about all those religious things, so I decided I really liked God. He was right behind Santa Claus at the top of my list of Good Guys. They both did a lot of good things, but Santa Claus was hard to top. He knew where every kid in the world lived and he did all of his good deeds in one night. I did give God a lot of credit for working all year long.

I learned a lot more about God and Jesus in Mrs. Bridwell's Sunday school classes. She explained that God wasn't really in the church listening to Homer with us, but he lived in another very nice place called Heaven. He was too busy running the rest of the world to spend a lot of time in Lone Tree, she said; however, he did make his only son, Jesus, available to teach us how to live good lives. She said Jesus was a Jew, but the world needed someone right away and Baptists hadn't been invented yet.

Everyone prayed a lot in church for things they wanted such as rain, good health, and high prices for corn. I wanted different things. I took turns praying to God and then to Jesus to help the St. Louis Cardinals win more baseball games. They must have been Chicago Cub fans because they didn't pay much attention to my prayers.

Granddad told me that most folks in Lone Tree, with the exception of Wilmer Blanton and Lorne Beasley, were good people. They were friendly and always helped each other during hard times, but Homer's sermons told a different story. According to him, everybody in Lone Tree, even Mrs. Bridwell, was a full-time sinner. His sermons left me feeling so scared and guilty that I had to make up extra sins so I could deserve all of the guilt.

The price of forgiveness for our sins was embarrassing and sometimes even painful. According to Homer, God wanted us to confess all our sins right there in front of all the people in church, and then agree to return the following Sunday dressed in our best clothes and be baptized in the cold and muddy creek behind the church, even if we had already done it. Granddad said that Catholics had a better deal. They were allowed to slip into a little booth where no one could see them and describe all the bad things they had done recently.

The dunking in the creek by Homer was guaranteed to wash away all of your sins, up to and including those committed that morning. Most people suffered through the ordeal because they were feeling real guilty and this was the only way to wipe the slate clean and start on a completely new bunch of sins.

Not going for forgiveness was worse because the penalty was a one-way ticket straight to Hell, which Homer described as if he had been there recently. It was a terrible place, Homer said, full of blazing fires and supervised by the Devil himself. Homer tried very hard to make Hell more frightening than baptism, but to me, a hot day in Hell didn't sound much worse than a cold day at the creek.

FIGHTING THE DEVIL

The struggle between good and evil was the normal state of affairs in Lone Tree. In fact, Granddad always used to say that Lone Tree was a favorite battleground for both God and the Devil because they both got a lot of help there. Everybody cheers for God, but they know that sometimes the Devil wins and terrible things happen. The Devil had his way when the river bottom flooded and the corn crops were ruined, but everybody had faith that God would retaliate the next year with a bumper crop of corn in the river bottom.

Sometimes the Devil would pick on one farmer in particular, such as the time when Leonard Green's Jersey cow died. But again, God seemed to be on top of things because two weeks later, his Holstein cow gave birth to twin calves.

Living in the eye of this spiritual storm seemed to nudge some folks in the direction of religion. Some felt that having Homer Allcock as the community religious leader gave the Devil a definite edge, so they were careful to give God all the help He needed to keep the Devil at bay.

Obviously, no one ever dared walk under a ladder or venture down a path where a black cat had crossed. These careless acts would bring on any manner of bad luck. Other thoughtless transgressions could cause more specific mishaps.

For example, playing cards on Sunday was a surefire way to go directly to Hell. Counting the cars in the funeral procession meant that you would get the next ride in the big black car.

During the winter, some kids would wear a little bag tied with a string around their necks. It was called an acidafidity bag and contained an assortment of foul-smelling herbs guaranteed to keep a variety of bad spirits and diseases away. It seemed to work well, maybe because anyone wearing one of these smelly little bags seemed to spend a lot of time alone.

Other beliefs and practices in Lone Tree fell somewhere between superstitious and highly unusual. For example, no one ever dug a well without asking Uncle Ferman to do his water witching. He could determine exactly where the well should be, and how deep to dig the hole.

Uncle Ferman's water witching consisted of crisscrossing the prospective well site holding both ends of a forked willow branch in his hands. He walked slowly gripping the magical twig tightly and holding it as far as he could reach in front of him. Suddenly, some unexplained force would pull the branch down pointing to the exact spot where the well should be dug. He would grimace as he struggled to keep the fork upright, but the little stick seemed to be in complete control. Some nonbelievers suggested that having a water table just twenty feet below the surface of the ground could have contributed to Uncle Ferman's spotless reputation as a water witcher.

Granddad had his own skills. His reputation as a wart remover seemed to have spread all over Greene County, so people with warts called on him from far and wide to improve their lives.

Granddad's simple procedure called for the patients to close their eyes and recite a verse of their choice from the Bible while Granddad rubbed the offending wart with a copper penny he had polished to a high luster on the bib of his overalls.

He never charged for his services so those demanding refunds had already been paid.

FIRES: JUST ONE OF NATURE'S TRICKS

Fires in Lone Tree were considered to be bad luck but just a natural part of life, like when the river-bottom land flooded. The nearest fire station was six miles away in Linton, and was manned by volunteers who might be busy with something else when a fire broke out, so farmers never depended on them for help. Also, one had to convince people to end their gossip sessions on the party line and allow you to call the fire department. The ashes were often cool before the Linton fire-fighters arrived.

The source of water for most farms was a hand pump mounted atop a well or cistern, so buckets of water had to be carried from the well to dump on the fire. This slow process taught everyone that the only way to keep your property from burning down was to prevent a fire, but if that didn't work, you had to be prepared to clean up the ashes and rebuild.

Mike and Goldie Soliday didn't have a phone, so when their hog barn caught fire they freed all the hogs and calmly watched it burn to the ground. Their main concern shifted from the loss of the barn to how to collect all the hogs before they consumed the vegetable garden.

Mike and Goldie's life would have been simpler without caring for so many hogs, but Mike had a serious love affair with them. Every fall he would buy as many hogs as he could afford, feed them throughout the winter, then sell them in the spring, usually without making a profit. When asked why he repeated such a losing practice, Mike would reply, "I know I don't make no money, but I do get their company all winter for free."

SUNDAY AFTERNOON BASEBALL

Homer Allcock's sermons on Sunday morning during the summer were longer than his winter sermons, which he justified by telling his congregation that people were out of doors more in the summer and therefore more likely to hide behind a hay stack or in the barn loft and go astray. Keeping twenty people in their pews an extra half hour could reduce sin in Lone Tree by a significant amount.

No one really believed that Homer had run this decision by God, but they all nevertheless left the church with an extra twinge of guilt. Even as their sweaty bodies lined the stuffy pews and their faces numbly acknowledged their need for Homer's sin-slinging sermon, everyone's mind was on the baseball game that would be played that afternoon in the pasture across from Saul Burchamp's store. The game was an acceptable place to release some of the frustration resulting from being unable to muster up a defense against Homer's sermon.

Most everyone would admit to a few common everyday sins, but they sounded so much worse when they were described, in detail, by the preacher in front of the entire congregation. Everybody except Homer believed that a charitable God would grant them enough slack to vent some aggression such as uttering a few dirty words, as long as it was confined to the baseball diamond.

Before the game could begin, the pasture had to be converted into a playing field. Several cows shared the pasture so bases were already there in abundance. It was necessary only to select the prize chips and arrange them in the form of a baseball diamond.

This challenge was proffered upon the umpire who reveled in the level of responsibility. As this was not a task to be taken lightly, the umpire always brought along his personal shovel.

The best bases were formed from cow chips seasoned enough to maintain high structural integrity but fresh enough not to break easily. Having a base break apart during a game could create a serious dilemma for the umpire. If a runner was standing on a chip that was split off from the main patty, the umpire had to determine whether or not he was actually on base. Very skillful chip selection would relieve the umpire of this weighty decision. Chips that were too fresh were also a hazard. No one wanted to slide into a third base that was too loose lest they have to go home and change their overalls.

The games were attended by everyone who lived near Lone Tree as well as the close relatives of those on the opposing team. When neither team could find another opponent they might play the same team two weeks in a row. The Lone Tree Cardinals played the Dugger Bull Dogs several times each summer.

Finding nine players was also a persistent problem. The standards of the Cardinals were such that a player didn't have to be very good, but just good enough so as not to embarrass the team or the spectators.

Very few skills that were developed on the farm helped in a game of baseball. Melfred Dailey was our player of last resort. He was called upon when absolutely no one else was to be found. He was a chubby young man with a pleasant round face and a head of unruly blonde hair. He had no natural athletic ability, as evidenced by the fact that he was fourteen before he mastered the art of milking a cow.

Only when no one else was available would Melfred be invited to play in right field. This was where he was least likely to have any contact with the ball. The Cardinals knew that any ball hit to Melfred in right field would be a certain home run, but they tried to keep this information from the other team. This was difficult when the two teams played against each other two weeks in a row.

Melfred's ability as a batter was no better than his talent in right field. He never actually made a hit, although now and then the pitcher might accidentally hit Melfred's bat with the ball.

Lefty Barnard had been born with only one arm, but he insisted on joining the team and developed into one of the best players for the Cardinals. Of course, with his handicap he had to develop his own style. It was pure poetry in motion to watch Lefty field a ground ball. He would catch the ball, toss it up in the air, take his glove off with his teeth, catch the ball with his one bare hand, and throw it to first base long before the runner arrived. Batting with one arm was a problem for Lefty, but he was still a better hitter than Melfred.

RADIO: CONTACT WITH THE OUTSIDE WORLD

Most of my contact with the world outside of Lone Tree depended on the quality of reception on our RCA radio. Its plain front boasted two knobs: a large one for station selection and a small one for volume control. From the few stations that could be heard clearly, most folks chose to listen to WLS from Chicago for the latest news. Radio WRN from Del Rio, Texas was the popular choice for religious inspiration.

About every five minutes Christopher Whipple, the evangelist who hosted the program, would blurt out a tempting offer to send you a Bible and a two feet high statue of Jesus for three dollars plus postage. An extra dollar would get you the deluxe model that glowed in the dark.

Norvel Haines had the deluxe model sitting on his porch, next to his swing. Homer Allcock took a dim view of this glowing spectacle and announced to his congregation that exhibiting the statue on his porch was no doubt a major sin and Norvel could probably look forward to spending eternity in Hell.

Norvel, who attended church only occasionally and always sat in the back row, had already resigned himself to being turned back at the pearly gates and he openly defied Homer's suggestion that he break the statue into small pieces and bury it in the woods. Nellie Gabbard sided with Norvel. At the next fish fry, Nellie was heard to say that the glowing Jesus on Norvel's porch was a more stirring religious experience for her than listening to one of Homer's sermons. The glowing statue of Jesus remained on Norvel's porch until the glow faded and the controversy subsided. My schedule for evening chores revolved around the broadcast times of my favorite radio programs, which lasted fifteen minutes and were offered once each week.

My day would be ruined if I missed a single episode of *Fibber McGee and Molly*, *Jack Benny*, *I Love a Mystery*, *The Shadow*, *The Green Hornet*, or *Captain Midnight*.

In *I Love a Mystery*, my three heroes, Jack, Doc and Reggie, would cheat death in some remote corner of the earth. I shiver when I recall their adventures in a cave in South America. It was inhabited by vampires, so my heroes spent most of their fifteen minutes swinging on vines from ledge to ledge to escape from the vampire cave with all their blood intact. Every episode would end in the middle of a swing, causing me to spend the entire week worrying about the safety of my heroes.

The Shadow always opened with the sound of a creaking door followed by an eerie voice that said, "Who knows what evil lurks in the hearts of men? The Shadow knows." The Shadow's edge on evil ones lay in his ability to make himself invisible. No one suspected that respected businessman Lamont Cranston and The Shadow were one in the same.

Granddad listened to the radio, too, especially the *Grand Ole Opry* on Saturday nights, but he was not a fan of classical opera. The one and only time when he tuned in to a station broadcasting an aria his only comment was, "I don't think that calf's gonna live."

HOME COOKING

The Great Depression was in full force and like everyone else my parents were completely broke, so Granddad once again stepped in by buying them a two-story, 600 square foot house on forty acres of land. There was also a barn and a chicken house but these would need a lot of help to remain standing much longer. The entire purchase totaled $1700.

Dad was unemployed, so we lived on government charity, plus help from Granddad, who would donate meat whenever he butchered a cow or a hog. The charity also consisted of groceries delivered to the house, such as flour, corn meal, butter, and lard.

During the deliveries, my job was to stand in front of the license plate of our 1930 Model A Ford. Having a licensed car would make you ineligible for charity. My ploy was never discovered, but I doubt that the people delivering the groceries were that concerned.

In those harsh times, food was judged more by its availability than by its taste. Some foods I liked and ate with zeal; others because they were the only dishes on the table. It sometimes helped for my sisters and I to close our eyes during meals, such as when Mom served up a mixture of hog brains and scrambled eggs with a big glass of warm buttermilk on the side.

This special Lone Tree dish was not as tasty as it sounds. We seemed to have an obligation to consume the brains of every hog my Granddad butchered. I think my mother added the scrambled eggs to try to make the hog brains more palatable and the buttermilk was added so we wouldn't have anything good to compare it to.

My mother convinced me that consuming all of those brains for years would make me smarter. I think she was right, because by the time I turned fourteen, I became too smart to eat hog brains and scrambled eggs. It took me an extra year for me to get smart enough to give up buttermilk.

CHRISTMAS: HAND MADE

During the Great Depression, Lone Tree was facing the same hopeless desperation that engulfed the entire nation, but we had a lot of experience with hardship. We knew times were brutal, but they didn't seem to be much worse than when the river bottom flooded and the crops of soy beans and corn were washed away, or when a drought caused all the crops except those in the river bottom to shrivel and die. The outside world viewed this era as bleak and devoid of hope. For the folks in Lone Tree, times were tough, but they were never willing to abandon the essential nourishment for their souls: hope.

The one thing we all looked forward to during this lean time was the Christmas season. It was a welcome opportunity to escape, if only for a little while, into a make-believe world where the improbable and the unattainable didn't seem so distant.

The family's Christmas preparations began with hitching the horses, Joe and Daisy, to the wagon and heading to the back of Granddad's farm in search of the perfect tree. By my seventh year, I was feeling grown up enough be a part of the adventure. My two younger sisters, Bonnie and Kibby, did not share my enthusiasm for the trek but they couldn't face being left behind so, at the last minute, they climbed into the wagon. After about an hour, they were cold and started whining to get back to the house and the fireplace. It didn't take long for Dad to weaken and settle for the first scrawny tree that was easy to cut and not too large to fit into the wagon.

Decorating the tree was also a family effort. All the decorations were handmade because money spent on tinsel would have come from Santa's budget for gifts and that budget was already paltry. Santa, we learned, was not immune to the effects of the Depression.

My sisters were fiercely competitive as they vied to see who could create the best angels, reindeers and Santas with scissors and paper. They also spent hours with a threaded needle in one hand and popcorn in the other making popcorn strings. My mother attempted to speed this process along because, until the popcorn was on the string, it was in danger of disappearing into the mouths of one of my sisters. Numerous unfortunate experiences with candles had convinced the family to enjoy a Christmas tree without lights, so our tree was most attractive during the daylight hours.

My sisters and I would compose our very important letters to Santa. The letters would include glowing reports of our good behavior and a detailed list of the gifts we had been dreaming about for months. Our parents advised us to be reasonable with our requests because Santa had a limited amount of time and many other houses to visit.

Christmas Eve was an exciting time. My sisters and I would lay awake listening for noises and pondering the many mysteries of the magic season. Why did the letters to Santa not require the usual three-cent stamp? How was Santa able to load all of the gifts for all of the children of the world on one sled? And if he did manage, how did those eight scrawny reindeer pull such a load? We worried that the roofs—especially ours—would not be able to support it.

We knew it was a selfish thought, but we hoped that, if an accident did occur, that it would happen after he had already visited our house. Despite our concerns, we remained confident that Santa would overcome the many obstacles and make his visits on schedule. After all, he must be very smart to remember the names of all of the children in the world. We knew that Santa would carry off his big night with grace, just as he always did.

As I grew older, I developed some serious doubts about some of Santa's feats, but I continued to play the game for the sake of my younger sisters. At times I even embellished the already tall tales.

With time even my youngest sister developed doubts about Santa Claus and all the stories that surrounded the Christmas season, but we all continued to play our parts during this magical time even after we ourselves became our only audience.

POLITICS

Serious political discussions in Lone Tree took place in the back of Saul Burchamp's store around a nail keg. There were only four straight-back chairs that were used by the checker players so any extra spectators had to stand or pull up a bag of beans. Sometimes Leonard Green or Porky Wadsworth would show up, but it was the McDonalds—Granddad and his two younger brothers, Dudley and Ferman—who dominated the sessions. When tempers flared, the arguments became loud, and if it was milking time, the session might end with the keg being kicked over.

My great-grandparents, the McDonalds, had raised the brothers with firm hands and a high regard for family values, but they still fretted over the possibility that, in a weak moment, any one of them could stray and do something crazy like marry a Catholic or a Republican.

Both Granddad and Ferman married nice Baptist girls from large families of Democrats, so family tradition was holding. Dudley was not married but no one worried that he would make a bad choice because he didn't seem to be interested in doing serious courting of any of the local girls. Great-Granddad George said, "I reckon that Dudley is of such a peculiar nature that marriage ain't likely."

The family was pleased when Granddad declared himself a Democrat and a devotee to Franklin D. Roosevelt and his New Deal. He was sure that President Roosevelt would bring the country out of the Depression and life would be better.

Family unity took a turn for the worst when Ferman announced that he had decided to become a Republican. Great-Grandma Myrtle fell into deep depression and announced that, "our own blood has gone bad." Ferman became more popular than ever around the nail keg as more people showed up to convince him of the error of his ways. He said, "Franklin Roosevelt's crazy ideas about this so-called social security will never work. I'm not willing to put money in a pot somewhere and trust the government to give it back when I get old."

Dudley, the youngest and the rebel of the family, declared himself to be a Socialist. No one had ever heard of a Socialist, but the family was delighted that they didn't have two Republicans. Anyway, with only one of them loose in the township, the Socialist wouldn't win any elections and it gave Dudley something to argue about.

The next heated discussion occurred when Ferman announced that he was going to run for the position of trustee of Smith Township. He said it was a big job, where he would be responsible for watching over the twenty-eight students at Prairie College Elementary School and reporting local road conditions to the county seat. He also had other important obligations at the school such as paying the teacher once a month and delivering a big pot of soup to the school every Friday noon.

Neither Granddad nor Dudley thought a Republican, especially Ferman, could handle this level of responsibility. Dudley suggested that even a good Socialist would have his hands full.

Ferman's only opponent in the election was Jake Tanner. He was a Democrat, which gave him a definite edge, but his reputation in the community became tainted when he sold Garber Norton a pregnant cow that never had a calf.

Folks in Lone Tree disliked Jake even more than they disliked Republicans and Ferman won the election with a landslide victory of sixty-three to twenty-five.

With time Granddad and Dudley's attitudes toward Ferman softened and they accepted him as the new trustee, provided that he allowed them to advise him on important matters. Since Ferman needed all the help he could get, he accepted their offer. The arrangement seemed to work well enough, and the keg was only occasionally kicked over.

THE FASHION SCENE

Deciding what to wear each morning before school was never much of a dilemma. I owned two pairs of overalls, two denim shirts, two pairs of white cotton socks, and a pair of durable shoes. My parents purchased these items for me every September and they were expected to last throughout the school year and well into the summer.

The process of finding church clothes was a bit more complicated and I had to rely on the generosity of my two cousins: Dick Clemens, two years older than me, and Beaner, who was just one year older.

The Clemenses had more money than my family, enough for the cousins to have Sunday clothes. When Dick outgrew his clothes, they were passed on to Beaner and when he outgrew them, it was my turn.

This would not have been a half-bad arrangement if the pants they passed on had not been corduroy knickers. These were baggy pants that came down to just below the knee and buckled around your leg. Wearing third-time-around pants didn't bother me, but wearing those sissy knickers was more than I could handle. I spent most of my time hiding when my Mother insisted that I wear them. Finally, my Mother took pity on me and offered a compromise. She would cut off the legs of one pair of pants and use them to lengthen another pair to make them into boy pants. They were still baggy and the material on the bottom of the legs didn't match the tops, but they were a lot better than knickers.

THE SOCIAL SCENE

My parents' spare time was scarce and money even more so, but occasionally they made time for leisure. They played cards now and then with the neighbors on a Saturday night. The men came directly from the field to wash their hands and faces in the enamel basin on the back porch, then on to the game. Bath time was normally on Saturday night unless you were having an early card game, in which case it was postponed until Sunday after milking time.

The women took off their aprons revealing the heavy cotton dresses they had worn all day and the men would remove their sweaty shirts and play in their undershirts. Usually the only food served was cookies or pie along with beer or iced tea. The card game ended early because everyone was tired and the cows needed to be milked at the same time the next morning even though it was Sunday.

Now and then, my folks would participate in a church social, a pie supper, or fish fry. The socials were potlucks with the women furnishing their favorite dishes. The only fare available at pie suppers was a large variety of pies and iced tea.

The fish fries were held whenever the river flooded the lowland near the White River. Farmers used pitchforks to collect fish stranded in the lower spots of the cornfields adjoining the river. The floods usually destroyed a portion of the corn crop, so fish fries were not always completely happy occasions. Lone Tree folks always accepted the forces of nature and they were resigned to having their fill of trash fish as meager payment for losing their crops in the land by the river.

QUILTING BEES

All quilting in Lone Tree began with the ragbag. When clothing such as overalls, long underwear, socks, or shirts became worn out, they were cut up and the useable pieces of cloth were tossed into the ragbag.

It took longer to wear things out in Lone Tree than it did in a big city. Overalls usually had about three layers of patches on the knees before they were relegated to the rag bag. Socks went into the ragbag only after you could slip them on from either end.

When the demands of the farm allowed it, the women of Lone Tree would assemble with their ragbags and have a quilting bee. Quilts were created by sewing together pieces of colored cloth from anywhere they could find them. Women would browse through one another's collection in search of the perfect rag. They seldom had a particular design in mind but were more concerned with finding a rag that was not too faded, not too worn, and exactly the right color.

Those in dire need of an extra cover on the bed before winter were entitled to the larger pieces of cloth, which helped expedite the process. Grandmothers usually had more time on their hands and consequently made nicer quilts with smaller pieces of cloth. The rule of thumb was, 'the older the sewer, the better the quilt.'

Those made for the hope chest of an unmarried daughter commanded the most attention. They would be pulled out for display whenever the parents of an eligible husband would visit. Sometimes, when a quilter was extremely proud of their creation, it might be entered in the county fair. If a quilt from a hope chest was shown too many times at the annual fair it usually was an indication that the quilt might be more desirable than the prospective bride.

THE FREE MOVIE

During the weeks of the long hot summer of 1939, folks in Lone Tree looked forward to Friday night and the free movie in Switz City. Late Friday afternoon, neighbors from other farms would gather in our front yard to wait to ride the five miles to Switz City in Dad's school bus. When he was awarded the contract to transport school children to Prairie College Elementary, he seemed to have accepted an obligation to haul a lot of people to town on Friday and Saturday nights.

The only site available for the movie was the vacant lot behind Miller's Truck Stop at the main crossroads in Switz City It was a good size, but would have been a lot better had it been covered with grass rather than black coal cinders. Most people brought a blanket or some feed sacks to lay over the rough cinders. A few fancy folks brought folding chairs.

Transforming a vacant lot covered with black coal cinders into an outdoor movie theater was not simple .The most essential item, the screen, was made from four bed sheets sewn together and mounted between two poles. Henry Crowder and Albert Shelp spent a whole day with their posthole diggers setting the poles. They had to be set deeply enough into the ground to prevent the wind from moving the sheets and causing the movie characters to move in an unnatural manner.

The projector was mounted on a folding card table about thirty feet from the sheets. Since it was a lot lower than the screen, viewers had to adjust to the idea that the top of the picture was going to be a little wider than the bottom. Thus, cowboys and horses appeared to be a bit top heavy.

The Friday Night Free Movie was the collective idea of the four business owners in Switz City. They hoped to increase business by perhaps selling more gasoline, hamburgers, Cokes, etc. Billy Sullivan, who owned the feed store, was not as enthusiastic, but he stayed open after the movie anyway just in case somebody wanted to take home a bag of ground corn.

On a good night, with good weather and a good movie, thirty to forty people would show up, including the dozen or so who climbed out of Dad's bus. Sometimes arrangements were made in school by puppy lovers to share a blanket on the cinders at the movie. Usually the girl would bring the blanket and the boy would bring two bottles of warm Coca Cola and an opener. Adults sometimes brought fried chicken or sandwiches and a jug of iced tea. No one drank anything stronger because the Baptist church was only about 200 feet away.

The movies were usually Westerns with an occasional Sherlock Holmes or Three Stooges. I liked the westerns with cowboys and Indians best. White people always portrayed Indians because a real Indian might not know how a movie Indian was supposed to act.

Sitting on cinders, drinking warm coca cola, and watching top-heavy cowboys was not for everyone, so probably more romances ended than started at the free Friday night movies.

GRANDDAD'S
BRUSH WITH SHAKESPEARE

Granddad made one effort to introduce the family to culture and enhance their social life. This Sunday started like most other ones with my parents taking my three younger sisters and me to Providence church for our weekly dose of religion, then on to the grandparents' house to spend the rest of the day. After church, Grandma and Mom were in the kitchen and Granddad and Dad were sitting in the big brown chairs in the living room absorbed in the Sunday paper. Granddad laid his pipe down and ended the silence by reading aloud an article in the *Linton Lantern* that told of a group of students from the University of Indiana who would be presenting a play called *Hamlet* at the Ritz Movie Theater in Linton on Sunday afternoon. The article described it as a tragedy written about three hundred years ago by some guy in England named William Shakespeare. Granddad reasoned that if it was called a tragedy it probably wasn't very funny, but if it was still around after three hundred years there must be something good about it. The paper described it as a cultural event and Granddad said that our family needed some of that. He wanted all of us to go to the play but everyone, including Grandma, balked at the idea of seeing something that old that wasn't even funny. Granddad was determined not to miss this rare opportunity to sample a little culture, so by 3 p.m. he was in his yellow Packard roaring down the gravel road on his way to the Ritz Theater.

He returned three hours later and sat through a long, quiet Sunday supper without even so much as a mention of his taste of culture. Everyone was curious about why he was so quiet, but no one wanted to be the first to ask. Was it so bad that he didn't want to talk about it, or was he just peeved at us for not suffering with him? Finally, Grandma broke the silence and said, "Well, Bob, tell us about that old play that you saw this afternoon. Was it worth the trip all the way to Linton?"

Granddad took a minute to enjoy the looks of curiosity on the faces around the table then said, "I never in my life saw anything that was that much work to watch. William Shakespeare, the guy who wrote it, lived in England a long time ago, before the folks there learned how to speak English very well. They used a lot of funny words that people don't use anymore. I had to listen real careful to every single word then leave out the ones that I never heard of and try to make sense out of what was left."

Mom wanted to know what kind of clothes these people wore. Granddad said, "I guess the actors were dressed like folks did three hundred years ago before they could buy stylish clothes from Montgomery Wards. The women had on long dresses bunched up in the back and a lot of ruffles around the neck. The men were all wearing pants that were about two sizes too small and shirts so big they were about to fall off.

"The main character, a young guy named Hamlet, lived in the castle with his mother Gertrude and his uncle Claude, the King. I suppose they had last names but they never told us what they were. They all seemed like people who would be real hard to get to know. I don't think I would buy a cow from any one of the bunch.

"No one in the family seemed to be very happy, especially Hamlet, who was having long talks with the ghost of his father. The ghost seemed to be about as strange as the rest of the family and kept raving on about how he had been murdered by Claude. He said that Claude sneaked up on him one afternoon while he was catching a little nap in the orchard and poured a big shot of poison in his ear that sent him away from earth without even receiving his last rites. That's a thing Catholics do just before someone dies. Without it he would be stuck in purgatory, a big waiting room for Catholics halfway between heaven and earth, where he would have to stay until things could be set right in the castle. He wanted revenge but he was just a ghost without a real body, so he asked Hamlet to help him do in Claude.

"Hamlet was not very good at making up his mind in a hurry and the ghost's request caused him to spend a lot of time saying silly things to himself. Once, right there in the middle of the stage, he just froze up like a bird dog on point, stared off into space and said, 'To be or not to be, that is the question.' I thought it was a little late in life for him to ask himself that. Maybe that was why he never gave himself an answer.

"It was about here when my head got so full of strange words that I got lost and nodded off for a little while. When I woke up things were really getting busy up there on the stage. Hamlet had finished off his future father-in-law with a jab of his sword and Hamlet's girl friend Ophelia had drowned, probably in the big round swimming hole they called a moat. Ophelia's brother blamed Hamlet for the whole mess and started a real fierce sword fight with him. During all the excitement King Claude and Queen Gert drank a shot of poison by mistake and bowed out of the action without doing much. In no more than five minutes after I woke up, everyone on that stage was either dying of poison or had been run through with a sword. Hamlet was the last to go, but after dragging it out long enough to do some more talking, he finally dies in the arms of his friend Horatio, the only person on the stage who was not dead and draped over a piece of furniture. Poor Horatio was left to tell the story, explain things to the ghost, and clean up the mess on stage."

Granddad said the feel of culture was nice but he would have liked the play better if William had given it a happier ending and hadn't killed off all but one of the actors. He said he didn't like that sort of thing even in western movies when Hopalong Cassidy does it.

FIREFLIES
AND LIGHTNING BUGS

When a moody spring moved aside for a soft summer, I always had a compelling urge to spend my time outdoors. I would even sleep outdoors.

It took three days to sew enough burlap feed sacks together to make the tent that would serve as my summer sleeping quarters. I erected it on the grassy slope between the back of the house and the vegetable garden. My younger sisters scoffed at my efforts and told me that my tent was the sorriest thing they had ever seen. I had to admit it was ugly, but to me, an eleven-year-old, it represented freedom, independence and an unmistakable sign that I was growing up. I fantasized that the tent was not fifty feet from the vegetable garden, but next to a raging river deep in the jungles of South America.

My summer bliss was shattered when my cousin, Junior Watts, came for a visit. I never liked Junior much, but my mother convinced me that God wanted us to love our cousins even if they were weird. I felt a little better after she told me the rule only covered first cousins.

I decided to make the best of it and invited Junior to share my summer sleeping quarters. He accepted my offer after I convinced him Davy Crockett had cleared the area around Lone Tree of all ill-tempered bears. Offering to share my precious hideaway with a cousin I could barely stand made me feel very proud of myself. I knew that saying nice things to someone you didn't like was something that grownups had to learn to do.

My spell of feeling good was shattered the next morning when I found myself lying on a very soggy blanket with Junior, who was still snoring. Junior had committed the sin of all sins. He had peed in my sacred place. He repeated his sin two nights in a row. I couldn't imagine how a blood relative could do such a thing. The tent dried out after my mother offered Junior a dime to get control of his bladder. Even so, the tent never seemed quite the same.

After Junior finally left, I decided to try to recapture the sense of bliss that Junior had befouled by sleeping outside rather than inside of the tent. I was alone in paradise with my dry blanket and the sweet odor of growing grass.

Maybe, in some mysterious way, Junior did me a favor. In the warm June evenings, the garden and the field beyond it were filled with thousands of lightning bugs. I learned later that city folks called them fireflies. I was spellbound, watching the little dots of light appear and disappear, only to reappear somewhere else.

I spent many a summer night gazing at this marvel of nature. My state of mind was so serene and forgiving that I even allowed Junior credit for his part in creating this wonderful episode in my life.

INDEPENDENCE DAY: COTTON CANDY AND SIDE SHOWS

The Fourth of July was a major holiday for folks in Lone Tree. In fact, it was right up there with Christmas and Thanksgiving.

The significance of this annual festival was nearly lost amid the excitement surrounding the arrival of the carnival in the Linton town park, six miles away. The town was not large enough to attract a larger carnival with more exciting rides and alert, bright-eyed animals, but it would be all ours for a day and we could hardly wait for it to arrive.

The carnival would have all of the wonders we had waited the whole year to see. A Ferris wheel, merry-go-round, sideshows, and a few geriatric animals suffering in the summer heat but doing the best they could.

The holiday occurred a few weeks before crops were harvested and taken to market, so most folks came up a little short of the amount of cash required to really let loose at the carnival. To meet this crisis, my mother would collect three or four hens that had not laid an egg that morning and sell them to Rolly Hollister, who came by the house in his mobile grocery store, called a huckster wagon, on Thursday mornings. Rolly's store was an old school bus filled with groceries. Crates for chickens were wired to the back of the bus.

No one wanted to come up short of cash and miss a once-a-year opportunity to experience any of the wonders of the carnival. Most folks felt that about three dollars would be needed just to be on the safe side.

Side shows cost a dime just to enter the tent, but once you were inside, you could incur an extra charge for something special such as a quick jerk on the bearded lady's goatee. The price of a fluffy mass of cotton candy was five cents.

Because my father drove the school bus, the entire community expected him to provide transportation to the event. By noon on July 4, twenty or more people would have gathered under the oak tree in our yard, waiting for my dad to rev up the engine of his 1935 Ford bus. No one ever knocked on the door or told Dad in advance that they expected him to give them a ride. It was understood that, "Them that's got, gives." By 1:30 p.m. the bus would be idling under a tree in the park in Linton and the excited passengers would come streaming out of the doors to commence the annual Independence Day adventure.

The array of attractions included a shooting gallery where, for a dime, one could take ten shots at little wooden ducks lurching across a rail in back of a tent. Knocking down nine ducks would get you a kewpie doll or a teddy bear. There were also booths where one could pitch very light balls at very heavy bottles. There were other tents for midget wrestling, the bearded lady, the strongest man on earth, and a person who claimed to be half man and half woman.

It cost an extra fifteen cents to lift his or her skirt and form your own opinion. Hickey Green always had those extra coins in his pocket to take a peek. He offered to describe what he saw for a nickel, but no one ever agreed to his deal because everyone knew that, had he seen anything interesting, he would have blurted it out for free.

The next day would be just another day on the farm, except that now they all had new memories to recall and embellish. Talk of the Fourth of July carnival dominated conversations for weeks, and Hickey Green never got a nickel from anyone.

154 *Lone Tree*

SWEET ROMANCE

In order for romance to blossom in Lone Tree, it was first necessary for the sexes to discover that they were different in some very basic ways. This discovery process was a slow and lengthy one for anybody who had not paid close attention to farm animals during mating season.

It was around the fifth or sixth grade that boys began to notice that catching a girl during a game of tag didn't feel the same as catching a boy. You found yourself hoping to sit next to a girl on the school bus, but usually regretting it after you discovered that sitting next to some girls made you nervous and feverish, as if you were coming down with the flu.

For me, Dorothy Hostetler was the worst. There was something about her that made me all jittery and nervous. I couldn't seem to say anything that wasn't silly. It would take three days to recover from a 30-minute bus ride next to Dorothy. My only real school bus affair was with Lorrie Loudermilch, but by the end of the semester we didn't like each other much.

The cooling of the romance began one snowy day when I went out to board the school bus. As was my custom on snowy days, I would do a little belly flop on my red sled and shoot down the slope in front of my house before boarding the bus.

One fateful day after an early spring snow, my show didn't go so well. The ground under the snow was not quite frozen, so when I did my dramatic belly flop the sled stopped abruptly when it rammed into the soft ground beneath the snow, but my lunch box and I kept going. We both tumbled end over end down the slope, coming to an abrupt halt next to the bus. I got up, brushed the wet snow and mud off my overalls as best I could, picked up my lunch box, and climbed onto the bus, but I was too embarrassed to sit with Lorrie. The next day she agreed to sit with me again, but the bloom was definitely gone from our romance.

The end of fourth grade was always punctuated with a play at the close of the school year. It was to be a two-person ditty with a boy and a girl, Rueben and Rachel, chiding each other. It began with, "Reuben, Reuben, I've been thinking what a great world this would be if all the boys were transported to far beyond the Northern Sea." Then the boy playing Reuben would sing the same message to the girls, suggesting that they weren't needed either.

To my complete disgust, Lorrie and I were cast in this year-end debacle. It was a losing proposition from the start for a couple of reasons. By now, we hated each other and neither one of us could carry a tune in a jug; however, because of pressure from the teacher and our parents, we gave it a half-hearted try. After about a week, both my parents and the teacher gave up. They got tired of us glaring at each other while trying to sing with our teeth gritted. They finally recast Ruby Harper and Thadius Spice for the ditty. They couldn't sing either, but at least they didn't hate each other.

Hay rides were an important part of the dating ritual in Lone Tree. Nothing could be more romantic than sitting next to a girl on a bale of fragrant hay while listening to the sputter of a John Deere tractor or the snorting, clopping, and flatulence of a team of horses. It was a magic setting where one could have romantic thoughts about someone you wouldn't even like the next day.

Before each hay ride, a group of girls who seemed bent on planning the lives of others would decide who would share a bale of hay with whom. The boys seldom objected to this arrangement, as their choices were limited to going along with the plan or sitting alone on a bale of hay in the back of the wagon.

Silas Owens was a problem. He drove the tractor that pulled the hay wagon, so it was not possible for him to share a bale of hay with the girl the matchmakers had selected for him, a winsome beauty named Leona Barnes.

A compromise was reached and the team of matchmakers decreed that Leona would stand behind the driver's seat while Silas steered the tractor. The arrangement worked out well. Everyone agreed that this romantic setting had contributed to Silas and Leona falling deeply in love. After all, Silas had allowed Leona to steer the tractor three times. To the delight of the matchmakers, Silas and Leona continued to court after the hayride.

To those who didn't know him well, Silas appeared to be relatively normal, but he was not very bright and his self-esteem was completely wrapped up in his 1935 Dodge sedan. Silas was not one to squander money on anything that didn't involve his Dodge, but he did spend twenty-five cents every Saturday night to squire Leona to the Cine movie theater. The twenty-five cents also covered treating her to a Coke and a hamburger.

Leona didn't seem to mind that many considered Silas to be the most tedious person in school. "That boy could talk all day about a stick, "Granddad used to say.

Leona was an attractive girl with a friendly face. She also filled out her overalls pretty well. Her main shortcoming was that she was extremely shy. Because Leona was so shy and Silas was so dull, it seemed inevitable that they would end up together at ice cream socials and other important events. Leona's family's hopes that she could do better than Silas were shattered when they attended the senior prom together. They were married a month after they graduated.

The perils of courtship were not limited to the young folks. A few of the more mature people wandered into this dangerous territory. However, having survived their youthful endeavors, their approach was decidedly more subtle.

The Widow Swaby's courting of Charlie Waggoner was so subtle that he never knew it was happening. Twice a week, the Widow Swaby would show up at Charlie's house with a freshly baked pie. Charlie loved any flavor of pie, so he never discouraged her.

The ritual continued for almost a year, but ended tragically when Charlie gained twenty pounds and succumbed to a heart attack. The Widow Swaby's next target was Homer Kemp, who also had a weakness for pie, and was very thin.

PUPPY LOVE

Robert Lundy was an eleven-year-old boy with a serious crush on my red-haired sister, Bonnie. Robert was very shy and appeared to be trying to hide behind the shock of unruly dark hair that would hang over his right eye. His hand-me-down shoes left a lot of room for growth, but the bottom of his pant leg had not touched his gray socks for months.

His painful shyness caused him to stare at the ground whenever he spoke to anybody, but his timidity was especially pronounced around girls.

Bonnie and Robert shared all the symptoms of a severe case of puppy love. They winked at each other in school and never missed an opportunity to meet at the water pump where they could share a drink of water from their personal collapsible cups. Both seemed to work up a fierce case of thirst about every ten minutes.

One Sunday morning, Robert showed up at our house on the pretense of having a strong desire to go fishing with me. According to Robert, a monster catfish in the pond at the back of the woods was waiting to outsmart the next fisherman willing to risk his worm and his reputation. I suspected it was a tall tale, but I decided to go along anyway, just in case he was right.

After I returned from collecting my fishing pole and worms, I noticed that Robert's attention had strayed from our fishing trip. He was standing in front of Bonnie staring at the ground while he toed little pebbles around with his oversized shoes.

Without a word, he reached into the deep pocket of his Mackinaw jacket and produced his version of the ultimate expression of love: a bullfrog about as big as a baseball mitt.

Robert was grinning with pride as he faced my astonished sister, her two hands now gripping his gift of love. After a moment, Robert finally spoke. He said the gift had spent all morning in the pocket of his jacket and he was sorry that it was drier than any bullfrog should ever be. Embarrassment claimed the moment as Robert and I hurried off to the pond, leaving my sister with her hands full of a very dry bullfrog.

By the time we had returned from our unsuccessful attempt to snag the monster catfish, Bonnie had regained her composure. She had eased the discomfort of the bullfrog by returning it to the creek where it could happily drench itself. She thanked Robert for the gift, but pointed out that, had the present been a flower, she could have pressed it between the pages of her English book and kept it forever.

My oldest sister, Kibby, also suffered through a short bout of puppy love. She was the main interest of Marvin Klug, a local boy with muscles as his primary asset. On Sundays, when farmers took time off for religious and social events at church, Marvin could always be found at our house.

He kept his mop of hair under reasonable control with liberal applications of hair oil. He parted it in the middle and combed it straight to either side. He believed that this hair arrangement made him a dead ringer for his hero, Jesse James.

Most folks thought that, except for his eyes being a little too close together, he wasn't a bad-looking guy. However, he was extremely slow to get the gist of whatever was going on around him.

Marvin never missed an opportunity to show off his strength to Kibby. Our family tended to exploit Marvin's combination of physical strength and mental weakness, and he became the major attraction on lazy Sunday afternoons while we sipped on a glass of iced tea on the front porch.

The routine began with Kibby remarking about his big muscles. After a few minutes of this, Marvin began to envision himself as even more powerful. In fact, his physical prowess was unlimited, and he could prove it. Marvin would prance around the yard, just like the stud stallions at the state fair. Kibby would gasp and giggle and declare that he was so strong that perhaps he could even lift the back of our Model A Ford. This was all that was needed to cause Marvin to puff up like an excited toad.

It wasn't long before he would strut onto the gravel driveway and stand behind the car, making a huge show of testing the weight of the car. As he postured, he would glance over his shoulder to make certain Kibby was watching. Then, with a mighty heave and a loud grunt, he would slide the car about a foot forward on the gravel surface. The entire family would clap while Marvin stood staring at the ground, embarrassed but bursting with pride.

We repeated this routine so often that it lost its appeal even for Marvin. At the end of the summer, his visits stopped and he turned his attention to the youngest daughter of the Gabbard family, three farms away. Kibby missed Marvin and the entire family missed the Sunday afternoon ritual. Kibby's broken heart mended when school started and she found a new beau.

After only one year of impressing Tilly Gabbard with his superior strength, they were married. They built a modest house on the back of the Gabbard family farm where they raised four children.

All were relieved to see that Marvin's talents were not limited to heavy lifting, but we were all convinced that his moment of glory truly lay in the moments he lifted our Model A Ford. After all, a man who can lift a Model A Ford can do anything.

HOME BREW:
GOOD FOR WHAT AILS YOU

During the era of Prohibition in the late 1920s, it was illegal to drink or produce alcohol. Telling hill folks they can't do something was reason enough for them to do it. Besides, their highly valued joy juice was a crucial commodity in their culture.

After the repeal of Prohibition, the hill folks continued with their tradition of making moonshine. They never understood why home brew was any of the government's business, and they resented any efforts to collect taxes on it. Consequently, the hills were dotted with stills.

The government agents assigned to root out and stop moonshiners, who were called revenuers and placed in the same category as varmints and Socialists. When squirrel hunting, one would frequently see a curl of smoke wafting up over the tops of the trees. We knew not to go there and take the chance of being mistaken for a revenuer.

The home brew recipe was usually made from corn or other grains and the still was constructed from copper tubing. The clear liquid drippings from the copper tube would be collected in Mason jars like the ones my mother used to store fruit.

The moonshine would then be sold, bartered for, or consumed by the same person who collected the Lone

Tree nectar in the Mason jar. It was typical for neighbors to gather in the evening to eat corn on the cob and pass the Mason jar around. Seldom did anyone have his or her own pint-sized drinking jar. It just always seemed neighborly to pass around a quart-sized jar. The communal jar also prevented any attempts to keep tabs on how much anybody drank.

If the session progressed into a second or third jar, the talk became slurred and the corn consumption became sloppier. At this phase of the party, attitudes about etiquette were relaxed and nobody minded the occasional need to pick a kernel of corn or two out of the jar before taking his or her turn.

At the end of the evening, there were only empty jars and a pile of ragged corncobs as evidence of this neighborhood social event.

DENISTRY:
TO PULL OR NOT TO PULL

Dentistry in Lone Tree was not complicated. The only decision to be made was whether the offending tooth should remain intact or needed to come out. If holding whiskey in your mouth for an hour or so didn't relieve the pain, the decision was to "yank it."

The care of children's teeth was also simple. The problem of a stubborn baby tooth was quickly resolved by attaching one end of a string to the tooth and the other to a doorknob. The first person to open the door solved the problem. Any concern about pain was quickly displaced with panic about when the door would open.

Serious dental problems were referred to Violetta Bull, Lone Tree's only dentist. Violetta was a powerfully built woman with a large head covered with unruly brown hair. Her thin lips and small, dark eyes were better suited for a smaller face. She always wore a faded plaid shirt with her overalls hitched up a little too high to appear comfortable. She seldom smiled and seemed to have little interest in appearing friendly and even less in appearing gentle.

There was some doubt among the local folks about Violetta's dentistry credentials. The more charitable gave her credit for attending at least a year or two of dental school. Willie Gabbard, however, was convinced that Violetta went into dentistry only after failing as a lumberjack.

Nobody knew her real story. We only knew that something had compelled her to purchase a used dentist's chair and hang up her shingle, declaring herself as Dr. Bull, DDS.

Violetta Bull became the dentist of choice for Lone Tree folks for a couple of reasons. For one thing, her office was conveniently located in back of the barber shop. Also, she would accept chickens, pigs and home brew for her services, and the only other option was to drive thirty miles to Bloomfield to a dentist who wanted to be paid with real money.

Dudley McDonald was one of the few whose experience in Violetta's dentist's chair motivated him to make the trip to Bloomfield. During the morning just before his appointment, Dudley swallowed the home brew he was holding in his mouth to ease his toothache and calm his reluctance to assume a compromising position in Violetta's chair.

After recovering enough to appraise the results of his encounter with Violetta, he realized that his aching tooth was still intact, but the one next to it was gone. It was common knowledge that Violetta also sipped a little home brew before each procedure to calm her nerves and improve her disposition.

Dudley blamed Violetta for the mistake, but Dudley's wife, Dora, was not sympathetic. She was of the opinion that Dudley and Violetta should share blame for the mistake because they both lacked the common sense to know that either the patient or the dentist needed to be sober on such occasions.

The next day, Dudley made the long trip to Bloomfield and paid real money to have his aching tooth removed, even after Violetta returned his chicken and offered to pull another one free of charge.

THE GHOSTS OF
THE WEATHERWAX SISTERS

I was about five when Angelina and Marguerite Weatherwax moved into the old house next to the Walker cemetery. No one knew where they came from, nor why two sisters would come to live in a dilapidated old house with nothing but a view of gravestones.

The sisters, who appeared to be in their sixties, had long coal-black hair and skin the color of skimmed milk. Their sharp features and dour expressions gave them the appearance of being intense, yet at the same time, preoccupied, maybe with maintaining their privacy in the midst of a nosy community. Their air of aloofness only intensified the interest of folks in Lone Tree. No amount of effort was too great if it resulted in a peek into someone's private life.

The reclusive sisters were seldom seen except when a curious passerby would spot them stooped over and hard at work in the large garden behind the house, or on Thursdays, when they made their two-mile walk to the Lone Tree Store to buy such ordinary things as sugar and salt. Angelina always walked slightly ahead of Marguerite. They both wore cloth bonnets on their heads, which were always bowed as they made their way along the side of the gravel road to the Lone Tree Store.

In a community where every day is a slow news day, a pair of mysterious sisters generated more gossip than busy people had time to process. Even the sisters' grocery list caused speculation. Why did they buy so much salt? How could anyone not need borax?

Three years after the sisters moved to Lone Tree, Angelina died suddenly. Because the sisters were seldom seen in public and had never asked for help, Angelina's death became public knowledge only when Marguerite walked to the Lone Tree Store and used the telephone to call the undertaker in Linton. Millie Pankey, the telephone operator and local gossip distributor, passed along the news to all of those in the community.

The funeral at Providence Baptist Church was simple and brief with a short, generic eulogy from Homer Allcock. The only attendees were Marguerite and a few local folks who were one part polite and three parts curious. Marguerite stepped up to the side of the casket where she appeared to whisper a final message to her sister. Then, she bowed her head and quietly returned to a pew far from everybody else.

Most of the hushed gossip at the funeral was focused on Angelina's hair. Her black hair had turned snow-white during her mysterious illness. Otherwise, the prevailing opinion was that she looked "purty natural."

Shortly after Angelina's death, Marguerite's black tresses also began to fade. Within a few months, her health had declined and her raven-black colored hair was completely white.

One morning, while delivering a bag of groceries, Saul Burchamp found Marguerite dead on the sofa, her arms folded across her chest as if someone had assisted her with her final repose.

Marguerite's funeral was a replay of Angelina's, except, with the spreading curiosity, the number of mourners had grown. The talk at the funeral centered on how unusual it was for both sisters to die so suddenly. Had they contracted some rare disease that would cause the color of their hair to fade and take their lives over such a short period of time?

The sisters had made arrangements to be interred together in a large, plain tomb located on the highest site in the Walker cemetery. It was the most prominent structure among all of the gravestones, becoming a permanent part of the cemetery skyline.

No one moved into the old Weatherwax house, and soon the broken windows and tattered shutters gave it the appearance of a haunted house. It was especially eerie on a breezy moonlit night, when one could hear the rattle of the shutters or the creaking of timbers in the old house, which loomed above the gravestones like the prow of a ship.

It became the perfect setting for the ghost stories that began to circulate around Lone Tree. Maude Tanner reported seeing two white specters gliding back and forth between the house and the Weatherwax tomb. Local speculation was that the sisters had unfinished business in this world, and everyone hoped that the completing of their tasks would not involve any of the local folks.

Nothing since the birth of the two-headed calf on the Callihan farm had generated gossip of such intensity. Beulah reacted to the tense situation by lapsing into a trance and receiving one of her frequent visions from the other side.

The Weatherwax sisters were part of a coven of witches, she said. They had been witches somewhere else where they were ousted from the group. This rejection, she explained, left them little choice but to go into exile and start their witchcraft all over somewhere else.

They chose to move into the old house next to the Walker cemetery and assume the quiet lives of retired witches, Beulah revealed. Beulah's vision was popular and she had numerous visitors curious about the information from the other side.

Russell Potter was the next to add to the speculation. Russell's vivid dream was a close second to Beulah's when it came to gossip fodder. Russell's otherworldly sources told him that the sisters had a rare disease which causes the hair to turn white prior to an untimely death and Lone Tree could be where the next world epidemic starts.

The postman, Walter Holt, was the only one to offer a thread of evidence connecting the sisters with a mortal existence. Walter respected the privacy of the mail system, but he didn't consider postcards private. He read all of them and shared the information with anybody who cared to ask what was new. Except for Beulah, Walter was the most interesting person in the neighborhood.

He recalled that, hardly a month prior to her death, Marguerite had received a postcard from Tilted Rock, Kentucky. It had no return address, but was signed 'Maude.'

The message was brief: "Cousin Wilma died last Thursday. We buried her on Moss Hill with the others."

This news merely added fuel to the inferno of speculation. Beulah started having more visions and Russell was dreaming on a nightly basis. The Weatherwax tales might have gone the way of most gossip and died a slow death had it not been for Bill Walker's annual trip to his family reunion in Oak Grove, Kentucky.

According to the dog-eared roadmap on Saul Burchamp's general store, Tilted Rock was just twenty miles due east of Oak Grove. It took very little urging to get Bill to agree to spend an extra day in Kentucky in an attempt to locate the mysterious Maude who had sent the postcard.

Bill had no trouble finding Tilted Rock. It consisted of about a dozen weather-beaten houses scattered along a narrow dirt road next to a creek. One of the hand-painted names on the mailboxes read "M. Weatherwax."

Bill knew he had found Maude. With his heart pounding, he walked up a dirt path to an unpainted shack with two homemade rocking chairs on its porch. A frail woman wearing a cotton dress and a cloth bonnet was rocking slowly in one of the chairs. She kept rocking, looking up only when Bill positioned himself directly in front of the chair.

She was suspicious of Bill until he assured her that his family lived just down the road, and they were practically kin. She told Bill that Angelina and Marguerite had been her older sisters. They were widowed and could no longer attend their farms, so they sold their land to the Peabody Coal Company and moved up north to Indiana.

She didn't seem surprised that the sisters had died or that their hair had turned white so suddenly. She said that a lot of strange things happened in the Weatherwax family and that she, too, felt a little "teched" at times. Some folks, she said, thought that it might be caused by too many kinfolks marrying each other.

Bill brought his news back from the reunion, but it didn't seem to excite anybody. His story couldn't compare to those conjured up by Beulah and Russell so it was soon forgotten.

STARTING HIGH SCHOOL

I was thirteen years old and feeling pretty grown up but also a little scared as I waited beside the gravel road for the yellow bus to take me to my first day of high school. I would be leaving Prairie College Elementary School with a total of twenty-eight students in all eight grades, to join a class of almost twenty freshmen at Switz City High School.

When I boarded the bus the first day, my friend Hickey Green was sitting alone in the front seat, so I joined him and we spent the hour-long ride staring out the window and talking about everything except what we were thinking. The older students were in the back being loud and making nasty remarks about the new crop of dummies. Hickey and I vowed that if we ever became upper classmen, we would be nicer to the freshmen.

The bus pulled up in front of the school and the older students bounded off leaving the rest of us to muster up the courage to follow. We gathered in a huddle beside the bus and exchanged nervous chatter until a teacher with a bun of gray hair and a kind face led us into the gym where we received our class assignments. Everyone started the year with Basic English, Algebra, Physical Education, and Social Studies. The girls were scheduled for Mary Snoddy's class in typing and the boys were placed in Henry Klopton's class in Agriculture 1.

The first two weeks were not as bad as I expected. I had new friends and the teachers were not as mean as I had been told. Also, I decided that I was not as dumb as my cousin said I was, and I might not fail all my subjects. Just when things were getting calm, a new crisis emerged that could be even worse than the first day of school. Friday night the school was having its annual back-to-school dance. It was an important event and everyone, even freshmen, was expected to attend. If you weren't there, it was likely that everyone would make up their own stories about why you didn't make it. The dance became the only topic of conversation. The girls were talking about dresses and the older boys were deciding whom they would ask to dance.

My concerns were different. How would I get there? Switz City was five miles away and Dad couldn't take me because he wanted to go to bed early so he could get an early start in the south cornfield. Also, what clothes could I wear to such a fancy affair? It didn't seem right to wear my regular old school clothes, so I would have to wear my church duds. I reasoned that if my brown corduroy pants and white shirt were good enough for God maybe they would be okay for the dance.

My first problem was solved when Hickey Green's older brother, Chancey, agreed to drive us to the dance and spend his time flirting with Midge Miller, the waitress at the Cross Roads Café, until time to pick us up. Chancey dropped us in front of the gym and sped off to see Midge.

After several minutes mumbling reassuring things to each other, Hickey and I entered the double doors. It didn't look like a gym at all. The lights were low, there was blue and gold crepe paper wrapped around the basketball hoops and long crepe paper streamers hanging from the ceiling. On the side near the bleachers was a table with a bowl of sugar cookies, a stack of paper cups, and pitchers of Kool-Aid and Apple Cider. Next to it was a small table for the record player and a stack of records. The chaperons, Mary and Marlin Snoddy, were already sitting in the bleachers sipping cider.

Some of the older students were dancing to a record of Tommy Dorsey's band, but the freshmen were still in a huddle at the edge of the dance floor. The boys were kidding and exchanging punches, while the girls were nervously whispering to one another. I thought the girls looked pretty good. They were all dolled up with extra lipstick, fuzzy hair-dos, and Sunday dresses. Maybe it was the lower lights or because they were wearing extra rouge, but I couldn't see any pimples on any of them, even Wilma Akins. I wondered if they could see mine.

Hickey said, "I'm goin' to ask Imogene Wilkins if she wants to try a slow one with me. Yesterday, my sister taught me how to do a dance called the two-step. She spent a whole hour with me and she said I was ready for anything." Imogene danced with Hickey but they didn't look that good to me. She was a lot taller than Hickey, and she made a funny face every time he kicked her toes.

Watching them helped me to conjure up the courage to try it myself. My mother had given me only one dancing lesson but I had practiced by myself for an hour in the barn. I couldn't do much worse than Hickey and Imogene. I only had enough courage for one try so I decided to ask a girl to dance who needed a partner so badly that she probably wouldn't turn me down.

The girls weren't in one group like the boys. The four cheerleaders were all wearing their gold and blue uniforms and standing together waiting to dance with basketball players. Most of the others were standing together, but two stood alone. One of them was Winnie Teller, who sat next to me in English class. She was very shy, had long brown hair, and didn't wear as much lipstick as the others, but she was kind of pretty for a skinny girl. She wasn't the queen of the class, but I wasn't Humphrey Bogart either, so maybe we were meant for each other, at least for one dance. After circling her three times, I finally asked her if she would try the next slow one with me. She accepted and there we were on the floor expecting the worst.

I was almost as tall as Winnie and we seemed to be able to dance without hurting one another. After two dances, I didn't have to count out loud and could even talk a little. The evening turned out to be less painful than I expected, and Winnie was nicer than the average girl. The last tune of the evening was called *Good Night Sweetheart* I danced with Winnie but it wasn't our best one. She looked at me a lot and I lost count three times. I wanted to come up with something really smart to say as we parted but I could only manage to say, "Well, I guess we got through that without hurting each other." She walked away without smiling.

I guess Clancy's flirting with Midge got old because he collected Hickey and me promptly at ten. We were barely in the car when he asked how the dance went. We glanced at each other for a moment, then told him that we danced like Fred Astaire and the girls were lined up waiting for their turn.

SWITZ CITY HIGH SCHOOL

Secondary education in Lone Tree consisted of a consolidated school that accommodated students from several townships. SCHS had more than a hundred students, but, many of them would be needed on the farm and leave school on their sixteenth birthday, one or two years before graduating.

Among the more memorable teachers from Switz City High School were Marlin and Mary Snoddy. They were hired twenty years before I entered high school and were as much a fixture as the battered desks. Marlin was the basketball coach and science teacher and Mary taught home economics, shorthand and typing. I didn't take Mary's courses because they were for girls.

Marlin was a huge, slow-moving man with a small, bald head that might have looked better on a smaller body. His major flaw was his inability to speak at a normal rate. Listeners became involved with what they thought he was going to say instead of the words that would eventually emerge during Marlin's painfully slow delivery. This was not a problem when Mary was around. She was always ready to read Marlin's mind and relate what he would eventually say.

Marlin spent most of his free time in the furnace room talking to the janitor, Russell Potter, who also spoke very slowly. He and Marlin developed a very close relationship that endured until Russell's heath forced him to retire.

Marlin's slow speech did cause a serious problem with his basketball coaching. Most time outs were not long enough for him to say much, so he spent most of the game sitting on the bench with his face buried in his hands. Only the top of his head was exposed to the players and the spectators.

When the team was doing well, his head would be a normal, flesh color, but when the team faltered, it would taken on a bright red hue. The way the game was going was pretty easy to guess from the color of Marlin's head.

The Switz City Switzers typically had a losing season. The team's dedication didn't quite make up for its lack of ability. The Coal City Miners and the Lyons Lions usually beat SCHS, but occasionally the locals bested the Jasonville Jayhawkers and the Worthington Whirlwinds. The Switzers weren't the best, but basketball was the school's only sport, and all the fans and students had faith that their day would come.

Ollie White taught history and civics at SCHS. He was a slight man with gray hair and heavy, horn-rimmed glasses. He was always dressed impeccably with a white shirt, a wide blue tie and one of his two suits. They were both gray, but one had stripes. He was ideal for his job because he was obsessed with the dates of historical events. Giving a wrong answer to Ollie when it concerned a date in history would earn you a disdainful stare that would make his left eye twitch violently.

Ellie Terhune taught girls' gymnastics and hygiene. She was a new teacher who was only three or four years older than the seniors. She was very pretty with long dark hair and a nice figure by Lone Tree standards. The freshmen thought it would be neat to have a mother like her while the sophomores speculated about her age. The juniors wondered if she bought her underwear from Montgomery Ward, and the seniors voted nine to two that she didn't own underwear.

Florence Pannert was our geometry teacher. Like the Snoddys, she came with the original furniture. She was a tiny, stooped woman in her early seventies. She wore thick glasses and sported a bun of gray hair at the nape of her neck. Florence would shuffle into the classroom every day clutching her notes, peering over her glasses as if wondering where she was. Her appearance and her yellowed class notes gave us the impression that nothing had changed in Florence's world for a very long time.

BASKETBALL:
ONLY GAME IN TOWN

The curriculum for boys at Switz City High School stressed the basics, such as agriculture, wood shop and basketball. We played basketball the last two hours of every day for the entire school year. The school had no other sports, so competition for a position on the team was fierce. Normally every boy over five feet tall tried out for the team and the others tried out for the job of towel carrier. I made the team more on my height than on my ability. I was the second tallest player who tried out.

In addition to me, the players were Jolly Moody, Vernon Roudebush, Dale Carpenter, Orval Newsom, Wayne Chipman, Russell Miller, Jimmy Justus and Gunnysack Landis. Our tallest player, Dale, was just over six feet tall. The only really tall people we ever saw were those in carnivals.

Gunnysack was a skinny little kid who couldn't throw the ball all the way up to the basket with both hands, so he only used one hand. He was also left-handed. Coach Snoddy tried for a year to teach him to shoot with both hands like the other players, but he finally gave up and allowed Gunnysack to have his way.

Gunnysack also had a very unique pair of eyes that worked to his advantage when playing basketball. When he was looking at you, it appeared as though he was also looking over your left shoulder. As a result, the opposing players always assumed Gunnysack was going to pass the ball to someone behind them. He became a very accurate shooter and it wasn't long before he was the team's highest scorer.

His peculiarities gave him gave him a definite advantage over the opposing team. Strangeness and limited ability were not enough to win all the games, but it helped, and most years we won almost as many games as we lost.

HALLOWEEN:
TRICKS BUT NO TREATS

Halloween celebrations in Lone Tree were very different from cities and towns. No one had ever heard of the "trick-or-treat" routine and the distances between houses made it impractical to walk from house to house. Instead, on Halloween, kids in grammar school would celebrate the holiday by coming to school in their homemade costumes. Bed sheets were readily available around the house, so about half of the kids came as ghosts. Most of the remainder came as vampires because plastic fangs were on sale at the drug store for those who could afford them.

The teenagers had a variety of favorite tricks such as placing outhouses or small farm implements on the roof of the elementary school. The more practical folks were puzzled because these antics were more of an inconvenience for the perpetrator than for those being tricked.

Those with more energy than foresight might turn over an entire field of wheat shocks, upright stacks of five or six bundles of hand-harvested wheat, which were bound together with binder twine. It was a small community where everyone knew the identity of the culprits. Therefore, the same teenagers who turned over the fodder shocks usually would find themselves righting them the next day in addition to their regular chores.

One of the most creative Halloween capers, although never repeated, was the painting of the genitalia of Fred Wright's favorite horse bright green. The horse didn't mind, but Fred was very upset. No one wanted to pay the full stud fee for a stud horse with green genitalia. The paint could be removed with turpentine, but the horse made such a fuss when this extreme skin irritant was applied to his tender parts that Fred just chose to let it wear off.

TRAINING TO JOIN THE SAINT LOUIS CARDINALS

It was a muggy afternoon when a sudden rain shower drove Leonard Green, his son Hickey, my dad, and me to the shelter of a big oak tree at the edge of the hay field. After the conversation drifted from fishing to talk about the future of farming in Lone Tree, I learned of my father's plans for my future, and they didn't include farming.

Leonard had already planned Hickey's future. He would buy the forty acres next to his farm from the Widow Swaby where he would build a small house and a barn for Hickey and any family he might have by then. Hickey seemed pleased with the plan of following in the steps of his father.

To my surprise, Dad said, "The farmland around here is not very good and it takes a farmer with real grit and fire in his belly to coax it into giving him a decent living. My boy may have the stuff to be really good at something, but I think he comes up a little short as a farmer."

Dad had never let me in on his plans but I remembered our family's failed attempt to find a new life in California so maybe he was offering me the chance that he never had for a life other than farming.

Dad was born in 1906 and grew up in the rural Midwest with little knowledge of any life except farming. He was only in his early twenties when the harsh times of the Great Depression descended on the entire country and life for almost everyone became a desperate struggle. Fate had dealt my father a life that required all his resources for survival and left little time or energy for fulfillment or improving his condition. However, he had chosen a life for his only son that was neither a continuation nor a repetition of his own, but one he would have had for himself if the opportunity had been his. He selected the only occupation he understood except farming.

He imagined that his only son would grow up to be a baseball player in the major leagues, maybe a star pitcher for the Saint Louis Cardinals. Dad loved baseball and never missed an opportunity to listen to an excited announcer give a play-by-play description of a game. He reminded me frequently that Babe Ruth was paid seventy-five thousand dollars for playing baseball for one season, which was the same amount as the President of the United States was paid, and Babe took the winters off and didn't have to run a country.

I liked baseball too, but my enthusiasm sometimes faded during the rigorous training sessions that Dad had designed to help me develop into a star. The exercise to improve my timing and control required the use of a discarded car tire hanging from a rope on the side of the barn. Dad would keep it swinging while I tried to throw the ball through the inside of the moving target. Just when I would be getting the hang of it, the tire would swing a little faster. I would be ready to give up but he would raise my spirits by repeating the Babe Ruth story.

For practice with a stationary target, Dad would sit with a catcher's mitt in the two-seater swing under the big oak tree in the yard. My task was to throw the ball to where ever he held the mitt while I pretended to be a real pitcher. This drill was fun except when I made a wild pitch and had to retrieve the ball from the field behind the swing. On bad days, I had more practice running than pitching. Coming back up the hill after retrieving one of my wild pitches was a low time when I wondered if anything was worth this effort and frustration, but once again Dad was there to remind me of Babe Ruth.

With time, the training became less humbling and more related to baseball. Occasionally, I was allowed to pitch an inning or two for the Lone Tree Cardinals on Sunday afternoons. Dad was the manager of the team, and he thought it was proper for a future star to play, even if he was a little young. However, he insisted that two conditions had to be satisfied before I was allowed to pitch: either the Cardinals had to be so far ahead that they couldn't lose, or so far behind that they couldn't win. After a season with no major catastrophes, I became the regular relief pitcher behind Lorne Beasley, who didn't really liked pitching, but since he had only one arm his choices were limited.

My high school could only afford the equipment for one sport and in Indiana nothing was as important as basketball, so I played the only game available at Switz City High. Shortly after my seventeenth birthday, my family moved to Phoenix, Arizona where, for the following four years, I played baseball at Phoenix

College and Arizona State University. I was an average pitcher, but not the star my Dad had imagined.

By the time the university training was over I had accepted my fate of never playing in the major leagues and, instead became a pitcher for the Phoenix Plumbers, a local team sponsored by the Valley National Bank. During one Sunday game I was delighted that all my pitches were working. It didn't matter what I threw. Sliders, curves, and fast balls were sailing right by the batters. It was as if all the batters had a bad case of the flu. It was the best game of my life. I was still reveling in my success when a man came out of the stands to ask if I was interested in a tryout with a farm team of the Cincinnati Reds. He said there were no guarantees but I would receive three hundred dollars per month for as long as I lasted.

Earlier in my life I would have jumped at the chance but things were different now. I was planning to continue to study chemistry in graduate school. I also realized that this was not a normal day for me on the baseball diamond. Even though I was only twenty-one years old, I mustered up the maturity to realize that this unreal day was just an echo of a fantasy that was already a part of the past.

When I told my Dad of this opportunity and my decision, the cloudy expression on his face reflected the disappointment of a shattered dream that he had nurtured for years. His son would never be a baseball player in the major leagues nor would he make as much money as the president. His only comment was, "Well, I guess this school thing you have goin' might work out, too."

BREAKING AWAY

My desire to leave Lone Tree took root the summer of my thirteenth year, when I spent unending days plowing the cornfield. That desire continued to grow as I matured and realized I was never meant to be a farmer.

My three sisters were too young to be concerned with such things and my mother had no ambition beyond fitting into the everyday rhythm of the farming community. But my father had dreams of a different life. We never spoke about it, but the faraway look he had in his eyes when he performed his chores gave him away.

Ten years after my family's aborted attempt to move to Bakersfield, California, my father tried once again to move the family to what he was certain was the Promised Land. With the urging of cousins from Bellflower, California, he persuaded my mother to move to the small southern California town.

Once again, we traveled across the country but this time in a 1941 tan and white Oldsmobile. My mother's cousin had rebuilt it from two wrecked cars. Shortly after arriving, my parents purchased a small house for about $4,500, taking out a mortgage for the first time in their lives. My father and I both got jobs with a tool company. I was fifteen-years-old, a year too young to work, but I was big for my age, so my parents signed a document swearing that I was a year older. We both were paid seventy-five cents per hour. I felt that was a fair wage for me but it seemed that my dad should be worth a little more. Didn't his thirty-five years on the farm count for something more in the world?

I wanted more for myself and the children I would have someday. I knew right then I would accept any job or perform any type of hard labor to pay for the education that I viewed as the only avenue of escape from my present life where the work of young men and old alike were valued at seventy-five cents an hour.

I donated the wages I made in Bellflower to my family to help with living expenses, but when the time came for me to return to school, which I was determined to do, we could no longer make ends meet. To their credit, neither one of my parents insisted I quit school, which many boys my age did back in Lone Tree.

Within six months, we realized we had once again failed at this new life. Once again, we were headed back to Lone Tree. Back to the forty-acre farm Granddad had purchased for us for $1,700. It was a loan, but all of us understood it would never be repaid.

My chance to get off of the farm came two years later when my aunt Jessie and Uncle Roy decided to pull up stakes and move to Phoenix. They offered to let me come stay with them and attend Phoenix Junior College. I jumped at the chance. My Dad's wanderlust kicked in one last time and my folks decided to move to Phoenix also. This time they made it, and spent the remainder of their lives there.

After a rocky start, I graduated with an associate degree in engineering from Phoenix Junior College and transferred to Arizona State University. My parents were in no position to pay my tuition, so I took any jobs I could find during the weekends and summers. I dug ditches in Ajo, a small border town in southern Arizona for one summer and spent the following one working on a water-drilling rig in Casa Grande, Arizona. I eventually earned a bachelor's degree in chemistry from Arizona State. I transferred to New Mexico Highlands University, where I earned my master's degree. I lived on the eighty dollars per month I made as a teaching assistant

A fellowship from Standard Oil of Indiana afforded me the opportunity to return to Indiana, this time to Purdue University, where I would pursue a Ph.D. in chemistry.

My studies came to an abrupt end two years later when the draft board decided I would be a perfect fit for the army. The prospect didn't appeal to me, so I immediately joined the Air Force as a research and development officer.

I married a fellow Purdue student in 1953 and commenced my new career in the Air Force. We were stationed the Army Chemical Center in Edgewood, Maryland, and I was now a second lieutenant. I had gone from watching fireflies in Lone Tree to witnessing the detonation of an atomic bomb.

In 1956, we were transferred to Denver to join a fledging effort called the United States Air Force Academy. After two years of teaching General Chemistry, the Academy sponsored my return to graduate school for two years and I finally completed my doctorate in organic chemistry at the University of Colorado.

In the years that followed, I rarely talked about Lone Tree. It seemed so far away, and I didn't think it was a part of me anymore. In 1970, at the age of forty-one, President Richard Nixon appointed me to be permanent head of the Department of Chemistry at the Air Force Academy. The U. S. Senate approved the appointment and promotion to the rank of Colonel. I retired in 1979 as a Brigadier General to accept a position with the Bechtel Corporation, which was building a new city called Jubail in Saudi Arabia's Arabian Gulf. It was a long, long, way from Lone Tree.

Two and a half years later, I left Saudi Arabia and accepted a position as Vice President of External Programs with Boston University. I spent the next fifteen years in Heidelberg, Germany; London, England; and Boston, Massachusetts.

I lost track of most of the people in Lone Tree, but my relatives always seemed to keep abreast of my activities, most of which confounded them. When he heard about Purdue, Arizona State, New Mexico State and the University of Colorado, Granddad shook his head and said, "Bobby Bill was always so smart. Wonder why it's taking him so long to get through school?"

Throughout my career, I carefully studied the mannerisms of successful people, and tried to behave like a person with a distinguished background. Everybody seemed convinced, but inside, I still felt like Bobby Bill with five nickels jingling in the pocket of his overalls to make him smile.

I didn't discuss my early life for fear that someone would find out I was an imposter who had no right to be successful. I feared the moment when somebody found out, and feared I would be sent directly back to the $1,700 farm where I would once again be a little boy standing in the cornfield.

With time—a lot of time—I realized that my years in Lone Tree were not an obstacle to overcome in my life. In fact, without the lessons I learned there, my life would have been something much, much less.

RETURN TO LONE TREE: VISITING THE GHOSTS

I visited Lone Tree in 1969, but not again until 2004. The tree that my Granddad always sped past on the left side was no longer at the crossroads, but the image of Lone Tree in the 1930s was as vivid as it had been sixty years past, when I stood in the same spot as a young boy.

Saul Burchamp's Lone Tree Store had been torn down, but as I stood on the lonely crossroads, I could see the rough wood planks of the porch and the red icebox replete with bottles of Coca Cola and Orangeade scattered over a mass of crushed ice.

At the other end of the porch, I could see a bluish, transparent liquid gush into the glass cylinder of the gasoline pumps as I pushed the lever back and forth while the level of gasoline rose. I helped Granddad measure out the two gallons it would take to keep the Packard running for another week.

I remember the shelves on two walls of the store were stocked with the basic staples—sugar, flour, and salt—but even more vivid are the memories are of the chocolate drops and sticks of hard, brown horehound candy shielded by the glass top of the candy counter. I could see the shelf above it contained an untidy stack of tattered comic books that were for sale for a nickel each, but seemed only to serve to entertain those nibbling on a chocolate drop or licking a stick of horehound.

Only a rusty water pump remains in the corner of the cornfield where my elementary school once dominated the scene.

The house where my youngest sister was born and I spent my childhood was torn down to make room for a silo. All I have left to confirm or discredit my version of that era are the fading memories of a few people who remain around Lone Tree. Most of those who remember the era as I do are gone, and the closed log of their unique memories will never be reopened.

During the last months before her death weeks before her ninety-third birthday, my mother seemed to go through a process of sorting through her most precious memories. She talked about them, but they were never recorded.

After an acrimonious divorce from my mother, my father and I had a minimal relationship for most of the remainder of his life. We finally reunited and both realized that our failure to communicate had diminished both of our lives. Four days after our reunion, he died. With him went all of the recollections that he had saved but never shared with his son. This sad, remorseful man with whom I had finally made peace bore little resemblance to the farmer and school bus driver I called "Dad" so many years ago.

The closest thing I had to a younger brother—until I realized she was a girl—was the next person I lost. Kibby, the little girl with the serious brown eyes that used to widen in horror at the prospect of a monster in the cornfield, succumbed in 2003 to an ill-defined disease.

I am the only person still alive who knew Kibby for the entire seventy years of her life. When I think of her, I don't see her at the end of her life—a frail, old woman with an oxygen mask, the only thing that lay between her and the beyond.

I remember a little girl with such complete faith in her older brother that she would ride her blind horse, Fred, while he was being led by his horse, Daisy, who had only one good eye.

I remember always sitting to the right of left-handed Kibby at the dinner table to avoid the pain she could inflict with her elbow. I remember how she never came home from our blackberry-picking adventures with blackberries, but with a purple-stained mouth.

I remember the primping ritual that preceded any dances or dates. By then, she had the help of her younger sister, Bonnie, who couldn't wait until she was old enough to be a part of the ritual. Our youngest sister, Janet, was at an age when she thought the whole primping thing was silly. Now, only memories remain of Kibby's seventy years of life, and I feel as though I am the sole guardian of all of them. The only tangible part that remains of her life is the fine ashes that have become a part of the sky and the beautiful sunsets over Mingus Mountain. For me, these sunsets will always belong to my little sister.

Bonnie and Janet, my two remaining sisters, have both lost their husbands—-Janet in 2001, and Bonnie in 2005. Bonnie's red hair is almost entirely gray now. Janet's is salt and pepper, and she looks so much like our mother, it's eerie.

Their versions of the past are different than mine, a story not uncommon between siblings who seem to have grown up in different households. There were others who witnessed the same era from a slightly different vantage point, but most are either not with us anymore or not inclined to record their memories.

The rate of attrition in the number of people and places to validate my memories is accelerating. During my visit to Lone Tree, I walked through the cemetery and saw the gravestones of so many who had been my classmates or relatives.

At the very front of the cemetery is the gravestone of Robert McDonald, Granddad. Just as he was a cornerstone of the community his entire life, he still remains in charge, no doubt barreling his Packard around the left side of any tree he chooses somewhere in the great beyond.

The world that once existed when my eyes were open now only exists when they are closed and on these pages.

ABOUT THE AUTHOR

Robert Lamb retired, after twenty seven years in the Air Force, as a Brigadier General. He has a Ph. D. in Organic Chemistry and spent ten years as the Head of the Chemistry and Biology Departments at the Air Force Academy. He then went to Saudi Arabia for two years as Manager of Training and Education for Bechtel Corporation in a project aimed at transforming a small fishing village on the Arabian Gulf into a modern city. The following fifteen years were spent as Vice President for International Graduate Programs at Boston University. He has published numerous articles on science and education in professional journals and gave lectures in India, Europe, and the Middle East. He now lives with his wife, Carolyn, in Puerto Vallarta, Mexico.

Made in the USA